Souls
by the
Sea

JENNIFER F. ARTHUR

Lulu Publishing Services rev. date: 01/17/2018

This book is dedicated to the ultimate dreamer, God, who not only puts dreams on my heart, but also fulfills them!

Chapter 1

"Love is a fantasy, love is a riddle."

She called her passionate. Francesca recalled back to conversations that she and her mother had when she was in college. These comments were in no way intended to be complimentary. It was generally uttered in a heated argument over the ever-enduring topic of her choice in an undergraduate degree. Francesca had no desire to be boxed in. She realized that if she didn't capitalize on her college education in a way that suited her, she was headed down the road to a neat little box with a pension at the finish line. Her life's desire was to use the stage as a means for expressing her passions, and her mother couldn't stand the idea of that. She wanted her to become a teacher, but the thought of making lesson plans and being cooped up in a classroom made Francesca's stomach crawl. She knew her major in theater, with a minor in French, was impractical. Her mother insisted she take Spanish, because it was more sensible. After all, they did live in Los Angeles. But sensibility was of no real interest to Francesca. She preferred to follow her heart and, much like the meaning of her name, she desired to be free. Everything she did was a silent plea for a life of adventure. On the stage, whether acting or reciting her poetry, she felt liberated and alive, even if, in part, it was a subconscious rebellion against her mother's pragmatism.

It was hard for Francesca to reconcile the fact that her mom, in her old age, had become so sensible. She was well aware of her mother's past, one riddled with recreational drug use, promiscuity and dropping out of college. Francesca reminded her mom of herself, minus the drugs and promiscuity. She saw Francesca's romanticism and free spirit as a potential threat to a prosperous future and fought Francesca every step of the way.

As the youngest of three girls, Francesca found it easy to flounder. Her older sisters seemed to always make "wise" choices, essentially choices that pleased her mom. Francesca reasoned that her mother had enough to be proud of in her sisters' accomplishments. Her older sister was an aspiring attorney and her middle sister was a high school teacher. Francesca felt no need to be something she was not, least of all, practical.

Aware that graduation was quickly approaching, she began to realize that her mother might have been right. Having started the job search in her last semester she began to see the evidenced futility of her choice, as she found no jobs that suited her. She had been on several auditions with local theater groups, and understood acutely that if she were going to make a career in theater she would need to move to New York. It wasn't like the thought hadn't crossed her mind, but being a child of the sun and the waves she knew that living in such a fast-paced city might crush her spirit.

The memories of her college years flooded Francesca's consciousness like a tsunami. She was tossed back in time after a recent phone conversation with her mother who had told her she was proud of her, and despite having thought she would never finish college, was overjoyed that Francesca now held the title of Assistant Director of Grants Management for the Department of Health and Human Services. It was hard to believe it had been seven years since undergrad.

Francesca slumped in her seat as she heard the voice on the intercom. "Please power off all electronic devices…" It had been almost a year since she had been home, and although mainly for business, she was thrilled. D.C. was nothing like California. With the exception of its ethnic diversity, people thought and existed very differently, and as she had feared, she was like a fish out of water as her west coast spirit was beaten back by buildings, trains and the bustling of city life. Frolicking in flip-flops during the summer and wearing a light jacket during the winter was more than appealing now that she lived in a business suit.

Now, living in the seat of the nation, Francesca learned she was politically moderate, which was somewhat rare since most people she ran across were either a staunch Democrat or Republican. She avoided political debates because she always felt too wishy-washy in her opinions, never wanting to commit to any one idea. However, when it came to human-itarian issues, she saw the world from the left, especially regarding race, inequality and poverty. While she had once envisioned her life expressing these topics through acting, she was now expressing her longing to help others through working with policy makers and nonprofit organizations. She liked her job, and although it was not as liberal as the stage, she felt she was making a difference.

Francesca's Libran need for finding balance was insatiable and she found it especially difficult to continue to maintain this balance in the capitol. Her theatrical literature professor, a bonafide hippy, once told her she was a walking anomaly. "You think with your left-brain, yet you're an artist." This was puzzling to him, but he remained intrigued by her points of view and frequent debates in the classroom. This dichotomous behavior was evident in many other areas, like her love of music and her concurrent fascination with silence. As a kid, she played flag football in the street with the neighborhood boys, but also had her fair share of Barbie dolls.

As the engine of the plane started, a chill overcame her. She pulled her jacket out from under the seat. It was summer time, but the chill was real. She knew the flight would be long. She was never good at sitting still for any length of time. She brought along some reading materials for her weeks' worth of meetings, but was disinterested. She gazed out of the window, the rush of the take-off made her heart palpitate. Her sense of adventure had not waned, yet she secretly hoped that with turning thirty, she would receive some reprieve from her tumultuous twenties.

Francesca reclined her seat after the captain assured the passengers they were at a safe cruising altitude. Her thoughts were rapid and restless; recounting the reassuring words of her boss who could not accompany her on the trip, but hoped she would be well-represented. Francesca thought about the parade of lonely nights she'd endured in D.C. and looked forward to this brief respite in her home state.

She convinced herself there was no time for love, although it was all she really longed for. In between first dates with stuffy men in business suits, she comforted herself with the rationale that her job was far too demanding for a real relationship. What man would want to feel like he was being penciled in?

For as long as she could remember she had been a dreamer and a romantic, but hadn't started thinking seriously about love until she was eighteen. She recollected a conversation with a college friend during her freshman year. Francesca had shared that, "All I want is to be in love." Like a knife cutting through butter, her friend rebutted, "Love is so hard and it hurts so much!" Since at that point Francesca had yet to experience being in love, she questioned why love had to be so hard. She wondered why growing up seemed synonymous with losing hope. Admittedly, now she was on the verge of believing she would be single for the rest of her life. While she wasn't completely committed to the newfound notion, her belief was based upon the fact that she had lost the love of her life, possibly forever.

Chapter 2

"Crashing waves beat down the doors of my inhibitions."

This touch-down was the smoothest landing she could recall. "Welcome ladies and gentleman to Los Angeles International Airport where the local time is..." She tasted the salt from her tears and hastily brushed them away. She could easily exhibit a wide array of emotions to an audience of strangers because they were the emotions of the characters she played. But when it came to her own emotions she was private, even keeping them from her family. Mostly because her sisters ridiculed her as a child, accusing her of being *such a crybaby*! Francesca's emotions ran deep, but over time she learned how to create a hardened exterior through humor and self-sufficiency.

She was looking forward to seeing Shannon, the one person who knew her inside and out. Shannon was the only person she felt comfortable enough to emote with. She met Shannon in college through a mutual friend. Initially she thought Shannon was dull, because she didn't talk very much, but after a few conversations she realized they had so much in common, like both being raised by their stepfather, appreciating the same music and their love for culture and travel. Shannon, however, was also very different from Francesca. She was even-tempered, an analytical observer, and played it safe. Francesca, on the other hand was full of spunk and always enjoyed meeting new people. She found Shannon a great audience because she could easily make her laugh. She often rehearsed lines for Shannon, who was enthralled by Francesca's acting abilities. "You are so talented." Shannon would tell her. "Why don't you try the big screen?" Francesca told her she preferred acting on stage because she liked the interaction with the audience. She also preferred stage acting to camera acting because she liked exaggerating. Shannon was more like a sister than a friend. She was always the first person Francesca would call, about anything. And right now Shannon's friendship was all that was keeping her afloat.

Francesca was glad she was seated near the front of the plane so she could easily deplane. She shuttled over to pick up her rental car, a Chevy Impala.

In-n-Out was her first stop. She knew this would become her tradition since they did not have them in the east. It was close to sunset, and having not seen one over the ocean for some time, she drove to El Porto. The ocean helped her feel calm, like a close companion.

She parked on the street closest to the bluff. Stepping out of the car she propped herself against the passenger door, crossing her legs and folding her arms as a sea of emotion crashed upon her. Realizing other motorists were there awaiting the sunset, she piled back in the car before completely losing herself in sorrow. Gripping the steering wheel, she sobbed uncontrollably. She hadn't thought about him much since she moved. Her longing for the ocean had often been tied to him. The only way she knew to escape him was moving nearly three thousand miles away.

———

They hadn't met like ordinary strangers. It was after a long day of work at the Marine Biology summer camp at the Alamitos Bay. Camp counseling was fun work. She spent most of her days kayaking, canoeing, swimming, and basking in the sun while leading a group of kids between eight and thirteen years old. At times she had so much fun she felt guilty for being paid.

She had pulled into her carport, like any other day when she noticed a man in her rear view mirror. Although she lived alone, she wasn't concerned much about her safety since that area of Long Beach was mostly college students and families. As usual, her car was filled with beach gear: a wet beach towel, lunch cooler, sunblock and a backpack. She kept her gaze on him while she gathered her things and stepped out of the car. Curiously watching the man dig through the trash, she figured he was searching for some lost treasure. He was well put together, in a rugged sort of way, and from what she could see, handsome. He had on a pair of light-colored jeans, a gray t-shirt, and some sneakers. His light brown hair was just past his ears and curled slightly at the ends. He had facial hair, a definite weakness of hers. She struggled to see his face. The way he was digging was methodical, not particularly frantic like someone who had lost something. During her examination she dropped her cooler and the commotion caused him to stop. He turned around and looked at her. Completely embarrassed, she collected her things and continued to walk toward her apartment. She took one quick glance back at him and realized he was still looking in her direction, his gaze inquisitive. She gave him a hasty, yet polite smile. He smiled back warmly. With heart racing, she quickened her pace. She never forgot his smile.

<hr />

Exhausted from the flight and her emotional exertions she threw herself on the hotel bed fully clothed and fell asleep. It was early in the morning when she awoke. The clock read 3:30 a.m. Frustrated that she could not fall back to sleep, she unpacked her clothes, hanging them immediately because she loathed ironing. Once she settled in, she scanned the room, admiring the contemporary decor and kitchenette. She'd made sure to reserve a room with a residential feel since she'd be here for a week. Since staying healthy and fit was always at the forefront of her mind, she had brought along some oatmeal, almonds, and dried fruit. All her life she'd had to work hard to maintain her figure and fluctuated between the sizes of six and ten. There were many men who liked her curvy frame, but the men she found herself attracted to often had a list of items for her to work on. Some thought her hair should be kept straight, but that took much too much effort since she was born with a full head of long, dark-brown curly tendrils. Others preferred she keep her nails polished, but she found that too exhausting and generally wore nothing more than a clear coat on her fingernails. Still others liked her to wear three-inch heels, but she felt most comfortable in sandals or flat boots. She didn't mind her short frame, besides, at 5'3", she would always be shorter than any man she dated. Despite these things Francesca had an incredible confidence about her. She scoffed at these men and was even so bold as to tell them if they didn't like the way she was born, perhaps they should look elsewhere. She did pay attention to fashion, and was generally well put together, whether wearing jeans or dressing for an evening out. Her style had a simplistic meets bohemian flare, and she never left the house without a killer pair of earrings.

She started the shower, but decided instead to take a bath. In graduate school one of the first things she was taught was self-care. Unfortunately, she was slipping back into some of her old habits, staying up late and not drinking enough water.

The bath water was perfectly mild, the way she liked it. She swirled the soap around to create some suds. Sliding into the tub, she sank back into her memories of him and the way they began.

———◊———

The face of the nameless man rummaging through the trash remained with her. The next couple of days at work were a haze, and then she had an unsettling dream. Much like her imagination, Francesca's dreams were epic; like a mini-series playing in her mind. Most of them never made much sense to her since they were a conglomeration of realities, conversations and memories. She always dreamed in color. However, to this particular dream she paid close attention. Not only did she remember the dream when she awoke, but it stuck with her for days. She dreamt she was in love with someone. Not just anyone, though. This was a young, attractive, and accomplished man who was homeless. The dream disturbed her and she wondered why it manifested. She thought maybe it was because she had been thinking about doing something meaningful with her life, and helping the homeless seemed like a good place to start. After mentioning it to a co-worker in jest and watching her raise an eyebrow, she never uttered it again.

Although she loved her job at the bay, it was only seasonal and she was starting to feel she was too old for that type of work. She was finding it harder and harder to find a job and began to feel like so many other recent graduates whose degrees seemed useless. She felt hopeless. As a means of escaping, she wrote:

Where do I belong? On another planet
or in a field of lilies that sway through soft breezes?
When does one know and how many places must one go?
Pace the countryside, the mountaintops, riverbeds, valleys below.
Someday I will travel the entire globe. Somewhere I cannot hide
from peoples' delight and God's awesome sights.
I'll try the cities, I'll dwell in the country. I know there is a place I will go
and dwell and feel and be. Maybe not on this planet, galaxy or realm, but there
is a place I will call home.

She couldn't shake the thought of the man digging through the trash and continued to wonder if she would ever see him again. It embarrassed her to think of him that way, but it was her only frame of reference. She wondered if he had found what he was looking for and why she hadn't seen him before. Perhaps he had just moved in. It was hard to keep track since there were over 300 units in the complex. She was attracted to his tall, lean build, his broad shoulders and strong jaw. She had always had a thing for sandy hair and light-colored eyes. His smile had been bright and genuine.

The dream of the homeless man also plagued her thoughts as she tried to make sense of it all. It prompted recollections of her American History class when the professor heatedly discussed some of Ronald Reagan's controversial policies during 1980s. He mentioned something about an attempt to reduce corporate taxes and making cuts to programs conservatives considered "big government". He continued on by saying that since he did not want to directly assault programs that aided people, who were often deemed lazy and criminal, he instead made all the decisions for the "good" of business. She was flabbergasted when she learned that as a result of his decree, nearly fifty psychiatric hospitals were closed with no recourse for the residents. She couldn't understand how someone could allow the mentally ill to end up in prisons or on the streets. After his poignant dive into these logistics, she remembered looking around the room to see the reaction of her classmates. Most seemed disinterested. Their response made her almost as upset as the lecture. It made so much sense to her now why so many people on the streets seemed "crazy".

After that class, Francesca started to do some research of her own. She discovered that many homeless people struggled with schizophrenia or other mental illnesses while simultaneously having combined drug and alcohol addictions or depression.

She conducted an informal interview with her stepdad, Sean, who was a Vietnam Vet, to understand his perspective on the issue. She was incensed to learn there were countless homeless Americans who were also Vietnam Veterans. They came back from war and were shunned by their fellow Americans, finding themselves without jobs, skills, families or support. She couldn't count how many times she had seen a vet on the side of the freeway asking for donations. Her eyes were being opened to the stark realities of her country. She asked Sean, rhetorically, "How could our nation send young men and women to war only to have them return to lives that resemble train wrecks?" She knew he did not have the answers, and it seemed no one did. She spouted, "We spend so much time recruiting soldiers, why don't we put the same effort into providing services for when they return, like mandatory mental evaluation and therapy?" She felt disillusioned.

Chapter 3

"Your smile is as refreshing as the smell of the Pacific and Atlantic oceans."

Francesca let out a sigh of relief. The weekend was upon her. It had been a long week at the bay. She'd had the twelve to fourteen year-old boys and, although they were her favorite group, they were tiring. There was a kid in the bunch she could have literally strangled. He was twelve, and rumor had it he smoked weed. He always had something to prove to the other kids and his insecurity was evident in his puffed up attitude and frequent bursts of rage.

The group spent the latter part of the afternoon canoeing. On their way back to camp they headed through the channel. Most times it was the hardest part of the trip because they had to paddle against the wind. In his usual display of "coolness," Milo stood up in the canoe.

Francesca said calmly, "Milo, please have a seat. That's not safe."

It seemed to be a sufficient warning because he sat and they continued on. No more than thirty seconds later, he stood up again. More agitated than the first time, she repeated the warning with firmness. Ignoring her, he began to rock the boat back and forth with a sinister laugh. Francesca could hardly contain her anger.

"Milo, if you don't sit down, when we get back to camp you're sitting out for the rest of the day, no questions asked!"

Seeing that she was agitated, he took the threat seriously and relented, to her relief. Although she was adequately trained, she did not want to have to fish four kids out of the bay.

Francesca's eyes dropped several times. She could barely stay awake for the short two-mile trek back to her apartment. To her surprise, as she drove up to the carport, she saw him. He must have been waiting for someone. The sun shone against his face, accentuating his golden tone. Her heart palpitated. She turned off the car and took the keys out of the ignition, but was frozen with fear. She looked at herself in the mirror and lamented the fact that she was such a mess. All day at the bay had left her with two coats of sunscreen and a residue of sand and salt water in her dark curls, which were arranged on top of her head in a messy pony tail. Her brown eyes, generally bright with enthusiasm, were droopy and tired. There was nothing she could do to correct her state. Resigned to that fact, she began to fret over other more important factors, like would she speak to him as she passed by, and if so, what would she say? She clutched her bag and cooler and got out of the car as if in complete control. He was leaning against a short post in her path. As she approached him she noticed something in his hand.

"Excuse me," he said. "I think you may have dropped this last week." It was a bottle of sun block. Other than an occasional case of sunburn, Francesca's light bronze skin did not blush, and for the first time she knew the heat in her face was not from the sun.

"Thank you, I was wondering what happened to that. Did you come all the way over here to give me this?"

"I don't live that far," he said. Despite his air of confidence he seemed nervous in answering the question. He couldn't figure out what was drawing him to her. It had been some time since his last relationship and he was not necessarily looking for another one, but something caught his attention the day he saw her. Maybe it was her long, dark-brown ringlets or her tanned skin. He liked exotic types and her almond-shaped mocha-colored eyes were intoxicating. Still, there was more to it. Perhaps it was the way she tried so hard to keep it all together the first day he saw her. When she dropped her things and muttered under her breath, it was apparent she was embarrassed and for that, he knew she was soft. Quite possibly, it was the way she looked him dead in the eyes, as if asking for his help, but knowing she could not. It could have been the way she smiled at him, although nothing more than harried and cordial, it lit up her face. He had always had a knack for reading people and he knew she was a good girl. Possibly a bit lost, but good.

"Wow that's very nice of you." She smiled and simultaneously began to inch away.

"It's no biggie. Like I said, I live close by," he reassured her.

"Where, exactly?" She inquired.

"Just up the street." He pointed with his finger.

"Well, it's good meeting you."

She felt awkward and wanted nothing more than to get in the house and shower.

Her state was far from ideal for meeting the man she'd thought about incessantly for a week.

"Maybe I'll see you around," he uttered tentatively, sensing her discomfort.

"Yeah, maybe."

"What's your name?" He asked.

"Francesca. What's yours?"

"Erick," he said with a half grin.

"Good to meet you Erick. I would shake your hand if I had a free one."

"That's all right, I'm sure we will have another opportunity to shake hands."

"Yeah." She giggled nervously. "Have a good weekend."

"You too."

She didn't know what else to say because while she was ill at ease, she did not want the conversation to end. She hadn't thought she would actually run into him again.

He had a presence about him, one of confidence and poise. He was a man and not a boy. He didn't seem self-conscious or pretentious. He had a slightly rough appearance, with his shaggy hair and simple style, but he was not completely unrefined. He was very well spoken. She couldn't help but replay the encounter over in her mind. They didn't even exchange numbers, how would she see him again?

———◊———

The bath water was getting cold. She looked down at her fingers and they had that look she hated as a kid. She knew it was time to get out of the tub. She glanced at her phone. It was 5 a.m. She couldn't believe she had been in the bath for almost two hours. Her eyes were heavy. Her morning meeting was in five hours. She climbed back into bed.

She was glad that, unlike many of her other business trips, she knew her way around. Her first day would consist of meetings in downtown L.A. She was scheduled to meet in the Ernst and Young building with a contingency of civic leaders from the surrounding districts, several non-profit homeless shelter directors, and the mayor. Following the meeting, the group would take a tour of the missions on Skid Row. Francesca sometimes felt too young for the role, but her masters in social work and urban planning, along with her passion, had landed her the job. The day's topic was gentrification, a word she had not even heard until graduate school. When she first heard it, she thought it was an epidemic disease. The words rung in her head as her professor defined it as "the process of renewal accompanying the influx of middle class people into deteriorating areas that often displaced poorer residents." In other words forcing poor people out of their homes so that developers can come in and build chic strip-malls and lofts. It happened way too often. She remembered thinking it would suck to be poor. She and her family were by no means rich, but she never remembered them worrying much about money. Poor people always got the leftover jobs, leftover homes, and leftover opportunities. Her professor continued with, "Gentrification is nothing new in a capitalistic society. It is simply deemed as progress, advancement, and the people who are displaced by commercial real estate developers are left to fend for themselves." This was the second time in her matriculation she could remember becoming angry.

As a kid, whenever she visited her grandmother for the weekend, they went to church. She remembered the preacher once quoting from the Bible, "The poor will always be among you." Those words continued to haunt her as an adult, but the sting of their reality made her realize she could not "save the world", although she might die trying.

The start of the meeting was a charge led by the mayor. Each person went around and discussed their role in the city and how they envisioned a homeless free zone. She was struck by one of the women's comments. Her name was Jane. She admitted that at one time she would never have envisioned herself working for, let alone directing, an organization that benefited the homeless. She confessed her past biases about the topic. Jane had porcelain skin, striking red hair and piercing green eyes. She looked out of place in the group that was so ethnically diverse. She told the group she never gave to a homeless person when they asked for money. She went on to say that she rationalized they would use the money for drugs. She said that growing up in a big city it was very easy to become disillusioned with the issues of poverty and homelessness and that she couldn't count how many times she'd seen panhandlers on the side of the highway with signs saying, "Anything will help" or "Have a heart." In the back of her mind she thought they were probably con artists and should get a real job.

Jane continued with a story about a lady in her mid-thirties who had boldly approached the driver side of her car in a grocery store parking lot. She was Caucasian. She told Jane she was hungry and needed food. Jane told her that she would have something for her when she came out of the store. She bought some Nutri-Grain bars and bananas and handed her the bag of food on her way out saying, "Here you go, I hope this helps." The woman's response took her aback, "Actually, I was hoping to get some money so I can buy some soup." Jane responded with, "I'm sorry, this is what I am able to give." She proceeded to her car, astounded, remembering the saying she'd heard numerous times as a young person, 'beggars can't be choosers.' She said she'd seen that same woman again on another occasion in the same grocery store parking lot, but she didn't recognize Jane. Her story was consistent; she had been laid off from her job and was homeless. Jane said she did not have nearly the same compassion as she'd had the previous time. In fact, she was annoyed. It was clear to her that the lady was on drugs.

Jane's ideals about homelessness were completely shifted when a close family member lost his job and he and his family were in the process of being evicted. She said it was her wake-up call to the fact that anyone could become homeless. They lived on the other side of the country, and she admitted to feeling powerless to help because she was not in the best financial position. That's when she realized it was not her job to judge.

The group listened intently and Francesca took copious notes. She assured the attendees that the federal money they were currently receiving would continue as long as the funds were available. She told them it was an honor to be there and to learn about how the monies were being used. The mayor spoke for the rest of the group about the services these viable organizations were providing from the federal dollars, and that the organizations were producing great results.

After their discussion and a gourmet lunch they made their way out of the building on foot, heading north on Figueroa and then east on 7th street. Not long after, they arrived at their destination.

She remembered it just as she had first witnessed it in her mother's car as a ten–year-old. Hundreds of homeless people lined up on the street. This time she did not feel the same fear she had back then, but the experience was still unsettling.

They were known as cardboard condominiums. Even police officers referred to them that way. For several blocks, thousands of homeless people resided on the sidewalks in their homes made of cardboard. Unfortunately, it was illegal to sleep on the ground, so every day at about 5 a.m. they were awakened and rousted by police officers. It was incredible that only a couple of blocks separated some of the nations most impoverished people from downtown's corporate district where slick professionals fully equipped with suits and lattes went about their business.

For the tour they had been advised to bring a change of clothes, jeans and sneakers so they would blend more easily. The mayor led the tour. Francesca wondered if some of the business people had any idea that these people existed. She imagined those who knew simply ignored their existence. But the signs were clear, even before entering Skid Row the downtown streets were crawling with homeless people holding cups and asking for change. The mayor stopped in front of the Midnight Mission. He began by saying, "Los Angeles, although only half the population of New York, has more people on the streets than New York has in shelters, and spends less than 10 percent of what New York spends for their homeless population. As of 2003, Los Angeles had approximately 40,000 people on Skid Row and an additional 45,000 in the greater Los Angeles area. I would like to be the first mayor to change these statistics." The group silently applauded.

A truck pulled up beside the group. A young man in his twenties stepped out of the car. He had on an apron. It was a Krispy Kreme delivery truck. He rang the buzzer to the mission and a middle-aged black man stepped out.

"Good afternoon, brotha." They exchanged an elaborate handshake. The young man returned back to the car and retrieved about fifteen boxes of donuts and handed them to the mission worker.

"Thanks man!" he continued, "You know, I'm feeling in a pretty good mood today, watch this."

No sooner had he placed the boxes on the ground than a crowd began to form. The man began to hand out donuts to the surrounding people, he handed some people only one, and others two or three donuts at a time. Then he stopped and turned to the group.

"Ya'll just gonna stand there or are you gonna help?"

Each group member hastily grabbed a box and joyfully handed out donuts. Francesca treasured the moment as one of the best she'd had.

The day was rewarding and productive, and Francesca was exhausted. She headed back to the hotel and plopped herself on the bed. Unable to nap and knowing she was only in town for a few days, she called Shannon. "Hey, what are we gonna do tonight?" Shannon was in the mood for Japanese food. Francesca was not one for turning down sushi. Shannon was coming from work so they would meet in Long Beach, for old time's sake. Francesca told her it was going to take a while for her to get used to her newly short, red hair-do. All throughout college Shannon wore her hair long, and since it was so straight it got a lot of attention from men. Shannon had a simplistic beauty. She was by no means plain, but she didn't fuss over her looks. Her alabaster skin was flawless, so there was little need for much makeup. She generally wore a muted lipstick and mascara which highlighted her curly lashes and hazel eyes. Shannon needed glasses, but always wore contacts, which she had traded in for some thick-framed retro glasses. She looked more grown this way, like a different person.

Dinner was delicious and the conversation was rich. Shannon talked about a string of bad luck dates she'd had with men her friends had set her up with. "Shannon, I told you, if you want to find a well-educated man who is interested in more than just his image, you need to move to the east coast. Plus, I can certainly use a good friend out there."

"Fran, you know I can't leave this job. I love working with the kids, and besides, it's one school district that pays really well. Unless I can find a job that is comparable, I am here for a while."

"I know, I know." But it was worth a try. I really do miss Cali, but I love my job, too."

"What's your day look like tomorrow?" Shannon inquired.

"Similar, but I'll be in Santa Monica."

"You know, I never understood how a city with so much money could have so many homeless people!" Shannon commented.

"Tell me about it. One city at a time."

They finished their dinner with a cocktail.

"Fran, you know I love you, if I could move to D.C., I would."

They hugged and Francesca watched Shannon get in her car and drive away. The sun had already set, but Francesca was compelled to drive to the beach, to the spot that had changed her life. It had been seven years, and it seemed like a lifetime ago. She drove to the bluff and parked at Cherry and Ocean. The oil islands were just as she remembered them, strategically placed, and illuminated like small towns. She sat in her car and looked up at the sign that read, *No parking after 10 p.m.* It was eight o'clock.

———◊———

"Why, hello there!" he said it as if they were old friends. It had been about three weeks since she'd seen him. She was just getting in from an evening out with friends. He was standing close to the carport, their 'usual' meeting spot.

"Hi," she replied, feeling a little shy at first. She was glad she looked much better than their previous meetings.

"I was in the neighborhood and thought I might catch you." The truth was, he'd made a special trip.

"I wasn't sure if I would see you again."

"What made you think that?" He cocked his head and gave a quizzical look.

"Because you didn't ask for my number."

"Yeah, I'm not much of a phone guy." He smirked.

"Me neither." She giggled.

"How have you been?" She didn't really know how to respond since they knew nothing about each other.

"Good, just a little tired. I'm definitely looking forward to the end of the summer."

"What is it that you do exactly?" Erick asked as he propped himself against the wall at the edge of the carport.

"I'm a day camp counselor at the bay near Naples. It's fun, but exhausting, especially with being in the sun all day."

"I can imagine. How long have you been doing that?"

"This is my second summer and probably my last. I'm starting to feel too old for it."

"And how old might you be, if you don't mind me asking?" He smiled.

"I'm not shy about it. I'm twenty-three."

"A mere babe," he said confidently.

"Babe? How old are you?"

"Take a guess."

"I'd say about twenty-eight." She was usually pretty good at making these types of estimates.

"Wow, you're good, you hit it right on the nose."

"Yeah, well," she shrugged with playful arrogance. Erick paused for a moment. He looked off to the side slightly, with a half grin.

"So Erick, what is it that you do?"

"I am a freelancer."

"So you work for yourself?"

"Exactly."

She dug deeper. "What exactly do you do for yourself?"

"Oh, a little of this, a little of that."

"Are you always this mysterious?" She inquired.

"Only when I need to be." He winked.

"That's all right, you don't know me. I imagine whatever you do must be really important."

"Top secret," he said with a big grin.

She laughed quietly under her breath. "It is getting pretty late, and I'm neglecting my cat."

"You have a cat?"

"Yes. He's my baby. His name is Oscar."

She had adopted Oscar from her mother who found him on the street when he was just a kitten and now he was full-grown.

"You go ahead and take care of Oscar and I'll be seeing you later."

"Ok mystery man. Until the next mysterious meeting."

"Cute!"

"I do my best." She winked.

"Until the next rendezvous then."

They walked in opposite directions. The sun had just begun to set. The interaction exceeded her expectations. She was under the initial impression that he hadn't asked for her number because he wasn't interested. Like previous exchanges, Francesca had no idea what to make of it, but it seemed like a fun game, and her girlishness, which she often kept tucked away, was being unleashed. She felt safe with Erick and safety was important, especially since some of the men she had dated in college were nothing of the sort. Her propensity toward the bad boy type had only left her feeling unfulfilled in her relationships. Erick was a breath of fresh air, no matter how infrequent their exchanges.

Before meeting Erick, the last thing on her mind was a relationship. Knowing that the summer was ending and along with it, her job, she was preoccupied with figuring out her life and career path. She was intrigued about what he did for a living. A freelancer could mean any number of things; perhaps he was a carpenter or an artist, maybe he was in advertising. Erick was more impenetrable than any man she'd known. It was like indulging in a soap opera, never getting the entire story, always left wanting more. She wasn't sure who to share this with, even her closest friends might be wary of such a stranger. She had no idea how to contact him, but she trusted they would see each other again, and soon.

Chapter 4

*"I saw an eagle today. It didn't speak a word, yet
left a loud impression upon my soul."*

It was Tuesday, her second day of meetings. She left for Santa Monica early so she could stop for coffee. She was one of the first to arrive at the recreation center where the meeting was taking place. A middle-aged Caucasian male greeted her. Rick was a little rough around the edges, yet she could tell instantly that he had a big heart. The plan was for him to give them a tour of one of the agencies that serviced the homeless in that area. Accompanying her would be several other homeless service non-profit executive directors, the Mayor of Santa Monica, and several local business owners, about thirty people in total. The mayor took the lead in creating a conversation between the businesses and the homeless services. The meeting's goal was not only for Francesca's benefit, but a chance for the business owners to understand the services being provided to the very people that, at times, were considered "nuisances" to them.

Once the others arrived, they had a light breakfast and proceeded on to the tour. Rick was passionate about what he called "his" mission. He had been the director for only five years after having served as Program Coordinator for their job programs and before that he was a client. "Over here you will see our beds. We only have fifty, so you can imagine how competitive it is to get a spot here. In other parts of the country, it is illegal to allow homeless people to stay on the streets during the winter. We find that the number of homeless people here in Santa Monica is so large because of the warm weather. Many of the people here are young, hippy types who perform their music or do art for money over at 3rd Street Promenade. Our program serves males, which is rare. The mission's goal is to offer job and rehabilitation services so that these men can get back on their feet as contributing members of society."

After the tour, the group sat in the meeting room. The mayor began by thanking Francesca for taking the trip out to witness the work they were doing. He also thanked all the directors and business owners for being present. He opened up an open forum for sixty minutes.

One business owner started. "I know that this is not necessarily a venting session, but I just have to start by saying that it's frustrating to have to shoo people off my stoop every day so customers aren't intimidated to walk into my store. You must remember that Santa Monica is one of the largest tourist attractions in the state, and when these people are impeding my business, it becomes very difficult to have compassion."

Francesca found it particularly challenging in these types of conversations to bite her tongue, but she remained professional. She remembered the time she traveled to Denver on vacation and saw a billboard that said "Lend a Hand, Don't Give", written in the palm of a hand to represent a panhandler. She felt the same knot in her stomach at that sign as she did now with this man talking about his bottom line.

The mayor did a fantastic job of mediating the meeting by allowing several of the nonprofit directors to share about the services they provided for the people. The forum ended with a discussion of the issues Santa Monica faced; with its paradoxical wealth and extreme poverty, it was one the mayor had to navigate very carefully. He admitted it was a struggle to find a balance when his constituents often complained about the "homelessness problem", but he knew the issue most likely would not be resolved within his administration and that he was doing all he could to alleviate some of the strains for all stakeholders involved. They broke for lunch and then had a series of team building activities and brainstorming sessions on ways business owners and non-profits could work together in the future.

The meeting ended around 5 p.m., and Francesca felt the need to clear her head. She took a walk along the promenade. She always liked seeing the street performers, especially the musicians. A large crowd had already formed as she walked up. She did her best to nestle herself into the crowd to see the commotion. There were two young boys no older than sixteen banging away on upside-down buckets. The music they created was fabulous. The rhythmic beats had the crowd moving their feet and bobbing their heads. It was just the distraction she needed as her heart continued to be heavy with the remnants of the day and the recollections of Erick. She squeezed her way through the crowd and placed a crinkled five-dollar bill in the basket that sat at the feet of the oldest boy. He smiled and nodded in acknowledgement of her gift.

On her way back to her car, a young man approached her.

"Excuse me miss, could you spare some change?"

Francesca rarely had cash on hand and had just given away her last bit of it. She told the man to hold on while she checked. In the corner of her wallet she was able to come up with two quarters and a dime.

"I'm sorry, but this is all I have."

"No worries, that's awesome, thanks, mam!" Before she could respond, he was gone. It pained her to give so little.

During college she had many thoughts on the matter and always wanted to be able to do more. She learned early on, however, that unsolicited giving could backfire. She recalled an evening in Long Beach, after she had enjoyed a meal. On the way to the car she saw a man digging through the trash in front of a nearby restaurant. It was clear to her he was looking for food, and as she approached, she felt compelled to hand him her leftovers. She was certain the gesture would be openly received. However, quite the contrary is what actually happened. The man turned his back on her and walked away. Embarrassed and ashamed, she never made the mistake again and concluded that people, homeless or not, still had pride.

She made it back to her car and clicked on the radio, but nothing moved her so she sat in silence. In the distance she could hear the chirping of sea gulls, and although it was only Tuesday, the city felt ready for the weekend. She stared at the Ferris wheel off in the distance; its slow, rhythmic movements were hypnotic.

———◇———

Feeling the need for inspiration in her job search, Francesca decided to take a walk to the park up the street. It was a Thursday afternoon; the weekend was approaching, but not quickly enough. Francesca walked slower than usual. Walking was one of her favorite past times. It helped her feel grounded and close to nature, and was perfect for deep thought and reflection. The sky was a perfect hue of blue with cirrus clouds strewn across like fresh car tracks in mud, but there was no hint of rain. Clouds were some of her favorite things. She became lost in them, thinking how she'd much prefer to live among them than on Earth, and imagined distant societies up in the sky. Her favorite clouds were cumulonimbus; she even liked the sound of their name. She continued to walk while looking up and saw a hawk circling overhead as she neared the park, assuming it was looking for some tasty morsel among the plentiful squirrels. She stopped and studied the hawk soaring on an updraft, marveling at the effortlessness of its wings as they never once flapped. She envied its unfettered life, unleashed of all complications or dramas, quarrels or heartache. She let out a deep sigh when she was reconnected with the reality that she would never be as free as a bird.

As she approached, she saw a man walking in the distance. He was tall and lean, with broad shoulders and a tapered waist. She was attracted to his athletic build and long effortless strides. The closer he got the more familiar he seemed. Before long she realized it was Erick. Francesca was completely caught off guard, and became self-conscious. Every other time she saw him she felt completely off-guard. Not as disheveled as she had been the first day they met, but she did not feel her best. Her hair was in an effortless ponytail and she was wearing gym clothes. Her curvy figure was toned by all of the summer camp exertions and her tan lingered, but she wished she at least had on lipstick. The closer he got to her the faster her heart pounded, as if she had just finished running to the park. It was not evident that he recognized her, and in an effort to avoid making a complete fool of herself she slowly drifted toward a park bench, still keeping him in her periphery. As Erick approached, he recognized her.

"Hello there," he uttered in his low, bass-like voice.

"Hello," she replied. Her stomach fluttered as he walked toward her.

"What brings you to this neck of the woods?" he asked.

Francesca let out a sigh. "I was uninspired in my job search, so I decided to take a walk."

"What type of work are you looking for?" he asked.

Something about the way Erick asked her questions made him seem genuinely interested, which made her feel comfortable.

"That's the problem, I'm not sure. My major was theater. I know it's not all that practical. My mom thinks I should be a teacher, but I'm not interested in that. Unless it's teaching high school theater."

"I think you would make a great teacher." He smiled.

"Really, what makes you think that?"

"You seem sweet and like you have a lot of patience with kids."

"Patient I guess, but not so sure about the sweet part." She grinned.

"Do you mind if I sit?"

"Ok," she acquiesced. They both sat on top of the picnic table facing the street.

"So Francesca," Erick turned his body slightly toward her, "Tell me more about what you think you may or may not want to do for work."

She let out another sigh. "I've always had a soft spot in my heart for people who are…I'm not sure how to say it without sounding snobbish, but people who are marginalized."

"Marginalized?" He cocked his head and squinted his eyes as if perplexed.

"Well, you know, people on the fringes, people no one else seems to notice."

"Go on." He leaned back and relaxed his shoulders as he placed both hands behind him on the table.

"I don't know, I guess I take notice of people whose situations seem less fortunate. That's part of the reason why I rejected my mother's prodding to become a teacher. I figured I would probably just end up paying attention to the kids who obviously had issues at home. But that's not the role of a teacher."

"Agreed, a teacher is supposed to teach."

"Exactly, and I have little passion for teaching, but I do have a lot of passion for people who are hurting. I notice I get excited about positions that are focused on helping people. I even took one of those job assessment tests. When I got the results, it said I should consider a career in Social Work."

"Social Work, eh? So you want to save the world?"

"I never thought of it that way, but it kind of makes sense. When I was a kid I loved animals. Every other month I was bringing home a stray cat or rescuing a bird that couldn't fly. My mother was so annoyed by it, but my stepdad let me be. He never said it, but I think my caring for these animals reminded him of his mom."

"Social work is one thankless profession."

"Yeah, I can imagine."

"What makes a good social worker to you?"

"Someone who is compassionate and not judgmental. Someone who people feel comfortable telling their most embarrassing secrets to, someone who cares about people, I guess."

"You guess?"

"No, I know."

"So I was right when I pegged you as sweet." He winked.

"Yeah, I was just testing you."

"You win." He had a gentle, yet strong way about him. He seemed much wiser than his years.

"Do you normally walk to this park?" she asked.

"Sometimes, but I much prefer the ocean."

At the mention of the ocean she lost him for a moment, as he drifted to another place. When he returned from his silent revelry she replied, "I love the ocean too. I take walks there a lot of the time." Her comment paled in comparison to his obvious passion.

"Maybe we can take a walk someday," Erick said.

"I'd love to," Francesca agreed.

"Just name the time and the date."

"Well, it's Thursday, August 5th, how about next Saturday, the 14th?"

"Wow, you're pretty quick with the math." Erick marveled.

"I do my best." She smiled.

"August 14th it is. Where do you want to meet?" asked Erick.

"How about Ocean and Redondo Avenue," she replied.

"Let's say 7:30 p.m., right at dusk."

"That's perfect," she said.

"Great." He gazed at her briefly and then turned his head back toward the street.

"It's getting late and I should probably head back to the house and get back to the dreaded job hunt."

Erick hardly disguised his disappointment. Francesca hopped off the bench.

"See you on the 14th." She beamed.

"Have a good weekend, Francesca." He slowly rose and waved as she walked off.

"See you soon, Erick."

She reveled at the sound of his resonant voice uttering her name. It was simultaneously melodic and harmonious. It sent a pulsing sensation from her head to her feet. Francesca felt so comfortable around him, as if they were long-time friends. His depth was what drew her. He had an ability to ask pointed questions that dug straight into her heart. She loved their conversations and couldn't wait until the next one.

Chapter 5

"I am dark and rhythmic, I like to bounce to the music in my car."

It was Wednesday, day three of the week's meetings. Francesca felt excited to hear from some of the most notable homeless non-profits from around the city. The meeting's focus was for each organization to give a presentation about their history, mission, services, goals, successes, and challenges. They would also share how they had been using the money from the five-year grant they all received. The meeting took place in downtown L.A., at the Omni hotel. The organizations spanned from greater Los Angeles to Long Beach and the valley, and were being represented by their executive directors. Francesca kicked off the meeting. She presented how the current administration sees the need to ameliorate the issue of homelessness in America and how these funds had been fought for through Congress. She told the group that while she had only been in this role for about a year-and a-half, that she had vision for the future and worked hard as the Assistant Director to continue to make these funds a reality for many other organizations. She alluded to Friday's gala, where the governor of California would address the group. She shared her elation about the fact that the money raised would go toward continued work and expansion of homeless service programs throughout the state.

The meeting was rich, and she listened intently to each agency's presentation. Her favorite part was when they each shared about the programs they offered. Many of the programs that supported homeless families had a requirement that participants save a portion of their salary each month in preparation of moving into their own home. There were other organizations that offered job training, drug rehabilitation, and programs for the kids.

During the intermission, between the first two sets of presentations, they had a luncheon in one of the hotel's ballrooms. The keynote speaker at the luncheon was the wife of the Mayor of Los Angeles. She gave a rousing and inspirational speech and presented a plaque of accomplishment to the organization that had been voted the most effective program for job placement, with the lowest rate of recidivism. Francesca's heart swelled with joy as she realized that the daily administrative duties of her job were becoming a reality before her eyes. These agencies were no longer just names in her database, but real people offering real services to real people in need. She understood, at that moment, why she had to be across the nation, away from her family and friends. Now it all made sense.

She had made plans to meet with her mother for dinner near her hotel. She headed back, full of hope and inspiration.

She was nervous and excited. Her date with Erick was upon her. She did her best to make herself presentable without over doing it. Her dark curly locks hung long when they were wet. Her brown eyes and golden skin tone was a far cry from the blues eyes and corn silk hair she was surrounded by in grade school. Growing up, she had a complex about her appearance because there was no one who looked like her in the neighborhood. It seemed like all the boys wanted the little girls with the flowing hair. Despite that her hair went clear down her back, it didn't flow; it was always pulled back into some sort of ponytail, braid or bun. Her complex continued through high school. She straightened her hair all the time, despite that when she sweated, her roots would always go curly. She even forewent working out so her hair would stay free flowing. It wasn't until college that she found the power in her chestnut curls. While taking a dip in the pool with some friends, her rubber band broke. As she climbed out of the pool one of her guy friends said, "Wow, now that's some hair! How come we never see it like that? It's awesome!"

Erick helped her to feel beautiful. It wasn't anything that he had said, but the way he looked at her.

She arrived at the bluff just as the sun was touching the edged of the ocean. Quietness nestled the shore. The amber glow of the setting sun reminded her of embers dancing in black coal. Her heart skipped when she heard her name. She turned around. The remnants of the sun danced in his blue eyes. She melted into her shoes as he gave her a warm hug hello.

"Have you been here long?" he asked.

"No, I just got here."

"Good."

"Shall we?" He led the way as they walked along the railing of the bluff. They both stopped to marvel at the sun's farewell.

"Man, I love that. The sun sets so fast, so powerfully." Francesca remained silent to allow the resonance from his voice to last in her ears. He had a way with his words. They were poetic and full of passion. His marveling at the sunset was innocent and profound all at once. She wondered how someone could have so much passion for something as simple as a sunset.

"Yeah, I know, it is so beautiful." His gaze lingered along the coastline as she spoke.

Erick turned his back to the ocean and propped himself against the railing. He faced Francesca and asked, "How was your day?"

"It was good and productive."

"Still on the job hunt?"

"Yes, but I'd prefer not to talk about that."

"I get it. What would you like to talk about?"

"What would you like to know?"

"I want to know everything." He smiled.

"Where should we start?"

"How about high school."

Francesca laughed. "That's a fun place to start, you first."

"Deal. Let's walk and talk. You mind?"

"Not at all."

Erick started. "Santa Monica High is where I went to school. There was this interesting mix of people and social classes. There were the really rich kids who lived up in the Palisades, Malibu, West L.A., and San Fernando Valley. And then there were those who stayed in Venice, Palms, and other lower income parts of LA. I was somewhere in-between. Although our home was in Santa Monica it was a modest house and we drove used cars. My father's frugality is what kept me level-headed and appreciative. We were surrounded by money, and had money, but never looked or acted like we did. My folks are simple people. I didn't appreciate it growing up, but now I can say that it is what shaped who I am today. Unlike some schools where kids of the same race would hang out with other kids of that race, we were actually separated by socioeconomic status. Thinking back on it now, it was really strange to me. I never really fit into the popular crowd. Outwardly I blended in, but inside I was much more about real people. I didn't choose my friends based on what they had, but on their ability to make a good time."

"What was your idea of a good time?" Francesca inquired.

"A good time for me meant adventure, which entailed adrenaline and uncertainty. Like the night my buddy, George and I, snuck into an Aerosmith concert. It happened on the fly. George was carefree. He was never concerned with what people thought of him. He was the class clown, but on the flip side, really intense. It was a Friday night and we had nothing to do. Before getting into the car I had no idea what the night had in store. I thought it would be our typical Friday, either bowling or shooting pool. We piled into the Nova that he and his older brother Steve had spent countless hours restoring.. He found out that Aerosmith had a gig at the Hollywood Bowl. Neither of us were huge fans, but it was something to do. On the night of the concert his intensity surfaced. George was a grocery stock clerk and I was working part time as a lifeguard for the city of Santa Monica. Since neither of us had a lot of cash we wouldn't have been able to afford the concert on our own, and I didn't like to ask my parents for money."

"Dude, I have an idea," George said. I knew his tone and the look in his eye all too well.

"Yeah, what's that?" I asked.

"Man, I heard there's an Aerosmith concert at the Bowl. I think we should go."

"George, man, you know I don't have that kind of cash." I had a feeling that comment was unnecessary, because I was certain of his response.

"That's all right, neither do I," he retorted.

"So what does that mean?" I played innocent.

"I know a way we can get in, and it doesn't involve money." George's eyes were wild with excitement. I was not the thieving or cheating type. I didn't necessarily go out and find opportunities like this. But when presented to me, I did not turn them down. Besides, it seemed more like a challenge than a means to a free concert.

"What do we have to do?" I was all-ears.

"Good, you're in, I thought you might wimp out."

"Wimp out! Not I."

"Although we were both seniors, George was older because he was held back in the 6th grade. I looked up to George, like a big brother. He had a maturity that made me respect him."

"What happened next?" Francesca asked.

"So as we approached the Bowl, my heart started to race. I was nervous and excited about our endeavor. I envisioned us scaling walls, climbing trees, and dodging security guards. I never once imagined that we would be hiking. Since the Hollywood bowl backs up to the hills, it's pretty remote. We parked the car in the most inconspicuous place we could find. The view of the city was amazing. I felt like we were on some important sting operation. The fence we crawled under looked like it had seen its share of concert pirates. I didn't think it would be so easy. We crawled under the rusted fence behind the stage and we were in. The crowd sounded like the rush of the ocean, as the concert was just beginning. We scouted out the best empty seats we could find. Our plan was that if someone came to ask for their seat we would just act confused, like we thought we were in the right seats, and then we'd search out another empty pair. The night was awesome! We ended up in the 15th row, right in the center. I'm not sure how we managed to stay there until it ended, but it was a night to remember."

"Oh my gosh, that sounds like so much fun."

"George and I had a lot of adventures like that. He was my only true friend in high school. We met in the 10th grade. We clicked because neither of us felt like we fit in."

"Did you play any sports in high school?" Francesca asked.

"Yeah, George and I both tried out for the J.V. football team. I was a competitive swimmer all through elementary and junior high and I thought it might be cool to do something different. I had good speed and agility, so I tried out for a running back position. To my surprise, I made it. After one season, I couldn't stand it anymore. The pressure to perform both on and off the field wore me out. I knew I was not the jock type. My athleticism always had a lot more to do with competing with myself than being a part of a team. I didn't like the pressure of having to please people with my performance. The coach and I really got along. He was disappointed when I told him I wouldn't be coming to practice after the summer training program. He told me of his plans to bump me to the varsity team that year. It was a tough decision, and although I was letting him down, I couldn't fake it any longer. I was not a football player. The rest of high school I just focused on my studies. I knew that if I got too distracted in extra-curricular activities, I wouldn't do well academically, and my father made it plenty clear that not going to college was not an option. It was plain to see that George and I were on two different paths. He wasn't motivated to do well in school like I was. He was from a blue-collar family and his dad stressed the importance of work much more than college. Fortunately our differences never came between us, in fact, I think it's what helped us stay friends. There was never any competition. There were times I had to be firm when he wanted to goof off and I had to study for a test. He would tell me, 'Man, you sure are dull.' When he realized he couldn't get to me with those jabs, he would leave it at that and say, 'All right, I'll see you tomorrow,' and then add, 'Good luck on your test.' I could always tell when he was disappointed, but he never pressured me to neglect my studies. During one of the rare times when he opened up, he told me he knew I would go far. I held on to those words.

George was street smart, but he also had this interestingly old-fashioned value system. He would talk about being a good dad and finding a good woman. He wanted to become a mechanic. If it weren't for the law, he probably wouldn't have been in school at all. It made me sad sometimes to think about graduation and what would become of our friendship, because I kind of knew that after we graduated our lives would be really different and we'd inevitably drift apart.

"Do you still talk to George?" asked Francesca.

"Oh man, the last time I talked to that character was a couple years ago. He's doing exactly what he set out to do. He's working in an auto shop and married a girl he met at the end of our senior year. He seems genuinely happy. It's hard to be a part of his life since he and Cindy have kids now. Being the single guy and having a married friend is pretty complicated, so I make sure to give them their space. Whenever we do talk, we just catch up on where we are in life and reminisce about the good ol' days." Erick stopped abruptly, "All right, you're up. Tell me about your high school days."

Francesca wondered why he wanted to change the subject so quickly. She reasoned that perhaps it was just too hard to talk about not being close with George anymore.

"To be honest, high school was a bore. I thought the kids were shallow and predictable. I went to four high schools."

"Whoa, why so many? Were your folks in the military?"

"No, between jobs, a new house, and divorce, coupled with my mother's nomadic nature we just moved a lot."

"How was that for you?" Erick asked.

"It was hard, having to start over every year. I was usually alone on my birthday, because it's in October, and I didn't have friends in time to celebrate. I hated moving."

"I bet. I can't imagine, since I lived in the same house most of my life."

"I have no idea what that feels like."

"You must be good at adapting."

"I think that's probably the only benefit for moving so much." Francesca rubbed her arms.

"Are you cold?" Erick asked.

"Kind of," she replied.

"What time is it?"

Francesca shrugged. "I don't know. I think we've been out here for at least two hours.

"Wow, time flies. I didn't realize I had been talking so much. I'll walk you back to your car."

"Ok." Francesca agreed, but wished she had never indicated being cold, because she really wanted more time.

"When can we meet again?" Erick asked.

"How about next week, the same time?"

"How about a little earlier so we can have more daylight?"

"That sounds good."

Erick walked Francesca to her car. As he waited for her to start the ignition he felt a twinge of disappointment seeing her go. He waved good-bye.

———◇———

Dinner with her mother was predictable, yet still, Francesca was glad to see her. They talked about her sisters and their accomplishments, and how her mom wished Francesca would settle down and find someone to marry because she wanted more grandkids. She assured her mother that she was fulfilled, and when it was time for her to find someone it would just happen. She had never been into forcing things.

While she appreciated spending time with her mother, she also looked forward to heading back to the hotel to get some rest since she was presenting to the group in the morning.

She was elated that tomorrow was Thursday and that the week of meetings was coming to an end. She would have the entire day to herself on Friday to prepare for the gala, which was taking place that evening. She decided that on Thursday afternoon, after her meeting, she would take a drive up the coast to Malibu. She had developed a fondness for driving up the Pacific Coast Highway a long time ago. It was the route her mother always chose when she and her family lived in Ventura. Francesca would look out of the car window at the homes on the hills, but dreamt mostly about having a house right on the water's edge. She would use the day trip to decompress.

The meeting started at 10 a.m. and took place at the Kyoto Grand Hotel in downtown L.A. She had chosen the venue herself, because it spoke to her appreciation for Japanese decor. This meeting was all hers, she would present the goals of her department for future programs and funding. Because of her background in theater, she did not fear public speaking.

She addressed the crowd of civic leaders, all thirty non-profits who had received funding, the mayors of Los Angeles, Santa Monica, Ventura, San Fernando, San Gabriel and Antelope Valleys. She felt prepared because she had written the speech before she left D.C. However, she quickly re-alized that after having been a part of the meetings, discussions, tours and experiences with these people that she would have to recreate it. The one she'd previously written felt too contrived. She reflected on the lives, stories, passion and drive of the people with whom she was partnering.

Francesca took the podium. She clasped her hands on the edges. She was certain to wear her tall shoes, being that she was only 5'3", they helped her feel more confident. This would have been the first time she took the stage, since college, but this time she was not playing a role, she was completely herself, and for the first time, she felt kind of nervous. She felt naked and vulnerable. Francesca let out a soft, long breath before she started to speak.

"I have spent the last three days with many of you and I realize something now. I realize that each of you is in this business for various reasons. You come from a multitude of backgrounds: civic leadership, non-profit management, program development, and some of you admittedly were once a client of the very organization that you are now serving. The single strand that binds you all together is your drive and passion to help a population of people who are often forgotten and seldom regarded. A population of people who most would like to pretend did not exist. Many of you have left corporate jobs to devote yourselves to this undying cause and for that, you deserve not only a round of applause, but the recognition that is rarely afforded you."

The crowd roared with cheers and whistles. Francesca led the applause and clapped while she scanned the crowd, ensuring that she looked each member in the eye.

She continued on. "My grandmother, a deeply religious woman, used to frequently quote this passage of scripture, 'To whom much has been given, much will be demanded.' As a child I had no clue what that meant, but as an adult, it started to plague me for the fact that I knew I had been given so much.

Most of my life I have felt a certain level of comfort with homeless people. As was evidenced to me by my ability to converse with them, listen to their thoughts and touch them. But simultaneously I can relate to those of you who so boldly shared about your initial biases and fears, as I too have found myself disillusioned, at times, by the issue. I remember when a classmate who was deciding to get her masters told me that she did not choose San Francisco because, 'There were too many homeless people.' As a young college student, I remember thinking that it was a good reason. However, now as I have been immersed in my role and have had countless encounters with the homeless, whether in passing conversations or serving on a soup kitchen line, it saddens me to know that it is still such a phenomenon in our country. Later, in college, I started to question what attracted the homeless to big cities. Why were some cities more compassionate to the issue than others, whereas some simply moved them around like jigsaw puzzle pieces or treated the issue like it was a plague? Los Angeles is a big city, with a large population of homeless. The work you have done and will continue to do is thankless, but crucial. You have done so much of the heavy lifting, and even still there is so much more to accomplish. The money you have been awarded through these grants is only the tip of the iceberg for what is still needed. We will spend the remainder of the morning discussing future plans and programs that the Department of Health and Human Services would like to see continue being implemented through future funding."

After her speech each mayor approached the podium and thanked the organizations for their role in changing the face of the city. They cited statistics on the number of homeless and how they have seen a decrease over the course of the year.

Francesca left the meeting with great satisfaction. This was the most rewarding work she had ever done. She looked forward to celebrating with the group on Friday.

She headed back to the hotel and packed a bag for her trip to Malibu, since she planned to stay overnight. She needed to be near the ocean and her hotel near the airport was making her feel landlocked.

As she had expected, Erick made it to the bluff first. The sun was higher, since it was only 6:30 p.m.

"You're late." Erick looked down at his wrist, tapping his pretend watch.

"I know, I'm sorry, I'm working on that. But since it's only five minutes shouldn't I be given a grace period?" She looked up with playfully apologetic eyes.

"All right, this time, but next time..." Erick mockingly scolded her. He reached out and offered her a hug, then took her by the hand.

"Ok, down we go. Let's walk on the sand this time, it'll be good exercise."

"Ok," she agreed.

Erick jogged down the stairs while Francesca took in the sites.

She counted aloud, "One, two, three, four..."

When Erick realized she was not close behind, he stopped and looked back up the long set of concrete stairs.

"What are you doing there, pokey?"

"I'm counting."

"Counting what?" Erick chuckled.

"Sail boats. It's this thing I have. I've done it ever since I was a kid. I have to count the sail boats."

Erick threw his head back and let out a roar of a laugh.

"Don't laugh, it's not like I'm obsessive compulsive or anything, I just have to count them."

"Well don't let me stop you, count away. How many are there?"

"Let me start over." With her finger she pointed as she counted, "One, two, three, four, five, six, seven, eight, nine. She stopped counting out loud and counted the rest under her breath. Seventeen, there are seventeen sail boats."

"What about those two over there?" He motioned to the other vessels in the water.

"Nope, those don't count, only sail boats, no speed boats or yachts."

"Hmm." Erick said under his breath.

"What?"

"Nothing, you're just interesting to me, that's all."

"I guess I'll take that as a compliment."

"It's definitely a compliment. I am interested." Erick smiled warmly to reassure her.

They made it to the sand nearest the ocean and headed south.

Erick started, "So last time we talked about high school, mostly my high school. You moved around a lot and went to four high schools. How about you tell me about your family?"

Francesca paused, and sensing her hesitation, Erick said, "Tell me what you feel most comfortable sharing."

It wasn't like she had never disclosed things about her life to her friends, but it wasn't something she talked about a lot. It made her feel vulnerable and she much preferred to be strong. She was ashamed to tell him that her father abandoned her when she was a baby and despite that she grew up with her stepfather, the abandonment by her own father played into so many areas of her life. And although she would never admit to being affected by it, one result was constantly seeking the approval of a man, while simultaneously keeping them at an arm's distance. But she couldn't do that with Erick. He unknowingly broke down her walls with his invisible sledgehammer. It was frightening and invigorating all at once.

She started with a long exhale. "My dad left my mom when my oldest sister was five. We're all two years apart and I'm the baby. At the time I was only one. He has never really been there after that, other than an occasional Christmas card when he knew our address. I grew up with my stepdad, Sean, who my mom met only months after my dad left us. We moved a lot, like I was telling you, mostly because of things like job relocations, and my mom and Sean's sometimes rocky relationship. They were separated a couple of times. My mom was really young when she had my oldest sister so there were a lot of growing pains. I know she loves us, but with all that was going on between her and Sean, at times she was impossible to live with. I couldn't wait until my 18th birthday because that's when I'd move out. My sisters and I aren't really that close. They thought I was strange because I was different than them. I was always day dreaming about a utopian society where everyone got along and I would often walk around the house talking to myself, always pretending to be someone else and carrying on full dialogues."

Francesca stopped talking for a moment and laughed out loud when she realized how silly she must have sounded to Erick. She looked up at him, but he did not indicate any sort of disapproval, so she continued on.

"It wasn't until high school that I realized all that pretending was me expressing my desire to be an actor, so that's why I chose theater as my major. My sisters are really accomplished, the oldest is in law school and my middle sister is going for her master's in education. I think sometimes my mom thinks I'm a lost cause since I majored in theater. She tried really hard to push me to be a teacher like my middle sister, but it is not who I am. My mother is much more practical than me, so sometimes we butt heads."

"What's your step dad like?" Erick asked.

"Well, he's a good guy, pretty straight laced, doesn't get his feathers in a ruffle. I think that's what my mom needed after our dad, who was an unstable addict. Sean is pretty emotionally detached. I find it hard to connect with him on anything deep really. We mostly just joke around. I think it's especially hard for him because we are all girls. He tries his best. He used to take us out to play football when we were younger. At times I'm sure he wished we were boys. I guess that's why I'm so tough."

"You're not as tough as you think you are." Erick nudged her with his elbow.

"What about your family?" she asked.

"I've been cursed with the "normal" family. Both my father and mother's parents came from Germany and made a stop in Minnesota. My mother's family moved to California when she was in high school and my father's when he was in middle school. Neither one of them is eccentric. They're both ordinary people with stable backgrounds. Aside from the fact that my grandmother endured much of World War II in Germany, there is not any sign of a spotted past. My father is a well-educated, hard-working engineer. He's never been the type to wear his heart on his sleeve, either. I've only seen him cry once and that was when his sister died. He's real even-tempered and doesn't raise his voice. His cool temper scared me growing up because I knew underneath it all, that one day he would lose it, especially with some of the stunts I pulled. I think I was encouraged to experiment with lawlessness because I knew my father had a long fuse. Even though I never did anything too crazy, I think I always felt this need to rebel against how stable my family was. Don't get me wrong, though, we'd have some heated debates, but they were just that, debates, generally around some political or social discussion, but always intellectual and always respectful. That's just it, as a kid I didn't respect how normal my family was. I thought it was boring. Especially when I got to high school and I'd hear about all the wild things my friends were doing or how dysfunctional their families seemed compared to mine.

41

At times I felt embarrassed to talk about my family. The one time I disclosed that my family and I always went to hear the philharmonic every Christmas George called my family The Brady Bunch. After that I kept all that kind of stuff to myself.

Personality wise, though, my mother is the complete opposite of my father, she's a pistol. She's not afraid to show emotion or speak her mind. Hers was the voice I would hear when she and my father argued. His low rumble permeated through the walls, but it was her high-pitched squeals that got my attention. Nonetheless, my dad wore the pants, and we all knew it.

"Do you have any siblings?" Francesca asked.

"I have a sister who's three years younger than me. Growing up we were inseparable. But when we got to high school she was not cool enough to hang out with my friends. She was quiet and smart and really sweet. She never got into any trouble. I respected my sister's strength to not be influenced by my sometimes-delinquent behavior. I don't think my parents had a clue about some of the things I got into, mostly because I kept my grades up. My sister, Pam, on the other hand, knew what I was like when I was with my friends. I remember one day, during my senior year, she came home sick from school and caught us sparking up a joint in the backyard. I will never forget her face. I couldn't do much to explain why I was in the backyard getting high, let alone ditching school. She never spoke of it to me or to my parents. Pam and I had this strange unspoken rule that we would never snitch on each other no matter what the circumstance."

"Wow, our families seem so different."

"Indeed, but isn't that what makes the world go round?" He smiled.

"Wow, look at that!" Francesca exclaimed.

The sun had created a pink glow against the few scattered clouds, as it set beyond the hills. Pink, purple and orange strands graced the sky.

"Only in California."

"I know. There's no place like it." The waves crashed, the silence was golden.

Erick turned from the sunset and looked at Francesca as she continued to marvel in the beauty of the sky. The glow of the sun gently painted her golden skin. Her hair moved tenderly with the gentle breeze. He had the urge to pull her close and kiss her, and for a brief moment felt his body moving closer to hers. He knew that even in these few conversations that there was something about her he had never experienced, a freshness and an innocence. He also knew that she was a woman. She was young, but she had a depth that was magnetic to him. Before meeting Francesca, the last thing Erick was looking for was a relationship, but he couldn't help the fact that he looked forward to their times together. He enjoyed the simplicity of their friendship, and while he was very attracted to her he did not want to move too fast. Every interaction was like a treasure hunt, and each new detail she shared about her life was a golden nugget.

"Francesca, when can I see you again?" The question sounded almost desperate.

"Soon, I hope."

"How about two days from now?" Erick asked.

"Ok."

"I am becoming fond of our beach meetings. Same time, same place, two days from now."

Erick walked her back to her car. He hugged her goodbye, but held her a little more tightly this time. Francesca could feel the difference in their embrace and was hoping for a kiss, but instead he released her and walked in the other direction with a simple wave. Francesca sat in the car, floating on the remaining essences of their interaction, confessing to herself that she had no idea what was happening, but she liked it.

Chapter 6

"If anyone can do it you can, strong as you stand, so grand, so grand."

Francesca could not get out of L.A. quickly enough. She took Lincoln Blvd. to where it met Pacific Coast Highway. She had spent her adult life learning how to avoid L.A. traffic, so she knew her plan was fool proof. She arrived at the beach side motel. It looked exactly the same as the picture she saw online. Having traveled the road on many occasions she never noticed it before. She knew her time before sunset was limited, so she hastily checked into her room. She didn't waste any time unpacking, but immediately stepped out onto the sand, which was only feet from her room.

Deeply, she inhaled. It had been so many years since she felt the way she did when she was with him. She missed his scruffy beard and his strong hands. She missed his smell and the way he could complete her thoughts. She missed him. Hot tears rolled down her face. The ones that so many times, in so many meetings, she'd had to fight back. She had done her best to hold it together, to not come undone, and it was now that she was able to unleash. Her sobbing could barely be heard over the undulating waves as she buried her head in her knees and wept until there were no tears left.

———◇———

Two days seemed like two months. This time she was on time. Feeling her presence, Erick turned around. He stood with his hands in his pockets, as if that would keep him from being overly excited. She loved his quiet strength. He was intellectual, but in no way stoic. Until meeting him, she hadn't realized how much she needed to be stimulated intellectually. However, unlike many intellects, he was very emotionally expressive, and there was something in his eyes that mesmerized her. They were full of hope and peace. His soul was old, but she could see the inner boy that was always present in their interactions. The depth of blue in his eyes reminded her of the ocean on a clear calm day absent of wind or turbulence. His eyes were honest and full of light.

"It's so good to see you," he said. "Let's head down, because I don't want to run out of sunlight." They walked along the bike trail.

"How was your day?" she asked.

"You know, the day of a freelancer can be tiring."

"What about you, your job hunt?"

"Never-ending." She sighed.

"Are you getting close?"

"It's so hard to tell, I apply for these jobs and then I don't hear anything. What I really need is to know someone in one of these companies."

"Sometimes that's the case. I'll keep my eyes peeled."

"Thanks, Erick."

"So, I know this is kind of a taboo subject, but I'm curious, tell me something about your dating life."

"Dating life?" Francesca raised her eyebrow.

"You know, past relationships."

"Wow, you don't waste any time." She laughed.

"I told you, Francesca, I want to know all about you."

"I'm not sure where to start."

"Wherever you want," he reassured her.

Francesca paused for a moment before she started. "My first kiss was during the summer of 9th grade." She snickered. "It was a girls' night, roasting marshmallows, swimming and hanging out. By this time I'd had a lot of crushes, but never a boyfriend. There was a group of kids at the next pit, playing football. Initially I paid them no attention until they began to inch their way closer to our site. One boy caught my eye. His name was Jonathan. He was mixed; Mexican and white. He was about 6 feet tall, athletically built, broad shoulders, sandy hair, hazel eyes and tanned skin. We casually began conversing and before long we found ourselves halfway down the beach. He was seventeen. I was only thirteen. As the night was winding down he invited me to walk down to the water so we could say goodbye. When I reached up to hug him, I was met with lips and tongue, but worst of all, I felt my teeth brush against his tongue and I thought, 'Oh my gosh, I'm a horrible kisser!' Francesca laughed. I wished I could have frozen time for a do-over. Jonathan lived about forty-five minutes away, and although we had a real connection I knew that it would be the first and last time I would ever see him." Erick listened intently as Francesca continued talking.

"With the exception of a couple of casual boyfriends in the 9th and 11th grades, I did not date much in high school. It wasn't until the summer going into the 12th grade that I met Pete. I didn't want to meet anyone that day; I just wanted to go on the rides. We were at Six Flags, not a place I frequented enough. Your sense of adventure involves adrenaline and so does mine. I love speed, and roller coasters are the ultimate rush.

"I met Pete through a mutual friend, at the picnic area. He hadn't asked for my phone number, so I was surprised when I received a call later that week. I learned that he lived about two cities away in the same county. Our first phone conversation lasted for three hours. I liked his sense of humor. Our times together were simple and fun. Our first date was at Denny's. He gave me driving lessons and we did donuts in an empty mall parking lot. It was really innocent. We both liked getting out of San Bernardino County, and in his father's truck we'd go to Santa Monica or Newport Beach. Although he didn't go to my school, he opted to go to summer school with me. We were taking different classes, but spent all of our breaks together. Pete taught me how to get high, on weed. I remember that day like it was yesterday. It was just before class. He took me to a park and we sparked up a joint. I took one hit and was ready to release, when he told me, 'No, hold your breath until you can't hold it anymore.' It took only two hits before I was completely high. I was so disoriented that I walked into the wrong class. When I finally sat down in the right class, I proudly and quietly proclaimed to my friends that I was high. They busted up laughing. When I told Pete that I told them, he scolded me, saying, 'Why did you say anything? You should have just sat back and peeped everybody.'

"Pete was really mellow. He had a super dry and sarcastic humor. He kept me laughing. Our relationship went strong the entire summer until just before the start of my senior year. Then he decided to move back to Philadelphia to live with his mother. We tried to maintain a long distance relationship and since it was before cell phones, the conversations were too expensive, so we only talked once a month. We maintained contact through my first year of college, but sadly I realized, after taking a trip to visit him, that we had grown apart. I was in college and he was working full time as a security guard. We ran out of things to talk about. We were no longer the happy-go-lucky sixteen-year-old-girl and eighteen-year-old-boy. On my flight back home I cried with the realization that our relationship was officially over. After that we lost contact. During college I had a smattering of unsuccessful flops, nothing worthy to be called a relationship. They were mostly men who I like to compare to sponges, you know, always taking, but not giving much back."

Francesca stopped herself in mid-sentence. She realized that the conversation could quickly go south, and judging from what she knew of Erick, he would want more detail. She wasn't ready to tell him about the men she dated, especially since many of them seemed like losers compared to him. In most of her relationships she was the giver, and the men the takers, but she was drawn to them because they were mysterious, dark, and intriguing. They gave her an intoxicating rush. She knew deep down they were not good for her. They were drawn in by her pretty face, voluptuous body, and charisma, but were never really interested in hearing what she had to say. She longed to have a relationship with a man she could share deep and philosophical thoughts with, a man that would appreciate not only her beauty, but her brains as well. At twenty-three she had already started to become jaded. Erick was different, he actually listened, and, although mysterious, he was not dark. He was resurrecting her belief in chivalry and genuine connection.

In an effort to redirect the conversation she said, "Enough about my relationships, I want to hear about yours."

Erick realized her desire to change the subject. They had already walked about a mile. Erick, as always, was keeping track of time, and said, "We'll walk a little more and then head back." He started his story. "I never had a serious relationship in high school. I didn't see the point really. George and I, however, didn't have a problem getting attention from girls, and most of the time it was unsolicited. George seemed a

48

lot older than he was. This, with his carefree attitude and goatee, was a real chick magnet. I, on the other hand, had the boyish good looks." He grabbed his chin and winked at Francesca.

"I couldn't grow facial hair at that time, and being a swimmer and lifeguard I didn't bother myself with hair products. Even with my messy, sun-bleached hair, I got attention. The kind of girls George and I attracted were very different. He attracted good girls, most likely because of his "bad boy" image. I generally attracted the artsy bohemian types. It was probably because of my shaggy hair and my tendency to hold intellectual conversations. The one thing I looked for in a girl was whether or not she could keep up with me in a conversation. Looks were important, but I didn't like the pretty, brainless type. Whereas most guys saw women as a means to an end, I saw them more as beautiful, mysterious creatures. Maybe it's because my parents, after twenty-five years of marriage, were still in love. My dad taught me that women were to be admired and appreciated. He always treated my mom with respect, even when she went off the deep end. My mom's passion made me nervous at times, especially when it was in anger. I think I've taken on a lot of my mom's qualities in that way, mostly her passion. It shows up in my love of music. Although I did well in school, I appreciate mostly my free and artistic side. In high school, when I wasn't hanging with George, studying or working, I spent countless hours playing chords on my acoustic guitar. I wrote several songs that I never shared, because I knew my friends would ridicule me for writing so many love songs.

Francesca stopped in mid-stride, looked up at Erick and smiled, saying, "I'd love to hear some of the songs you've written." He looked down at her warmly and continued on.

"It wasn't until college, when I met my first serious girlfriend, that I felt comfortable enough to let my creative side show. She helped me to feel at ease. She was an intellectual, and she appreciated my talents. Most of our time together was spent discussing philosophy, politics, and social change while sitting in remote places on campus. Berkeley gave me a chance to get out of my comfort zone and gain some perspective. I felt like people in southern California were clueless when it came to anything real, like social justice and how the government works. I don't proclaim to be a political buff, nor do I venture to say I'm a radical. But,

I have strong opinions on things, and knew that L.A. was not the place to express them. But, I didn't want to be too far from home. Northern California seemed like a different planet to me, and Patricia was completely different from the girls I experienced in high school. She was refreshingly unselfconscious, which was surprising to me, because she was beautiful. She was a brunette, and her eyes were the color of brown sugar.

"The first time I saw her was in our political science class. She was sitting on the other side of the lecture hall. I remember her long hair, and the clothes she was wearing made her look soft. I noticed her after she raised her hand and asked the professor what his opinion was of the flux of homeless people in America and if he thought Ronald Reagan's decision to close down mental health institutions was the direct cause. I could tell he was caught off guard by her question. I looked at her for her reaction. She didn't seem impatient with the professor at all. Instead, she waited, with a soft look of compassion. I knew at that moment I needed to know her name. After class I hurried to the top of the stairs and waited for her, pretending I was waiting for a friend. I causally said to her, "Great question in class. What made you ask that?" She went into a story about her cousin whose father was a Vietnam vet and after coming back from the war was totally wigged out. He never assimilated back into society, and the mental health care for veterans was less than ideal. I cared less about what she said and more about the passion with which she said it.

"After that first meeting, I made it a point to sit closer to her. Finally we began sitting next to one another and going for coffee after class. We spent hours talking about things that we wanted to see differently in the world. I knew from the beginning that she was much more passionate about those things than I was, but our conversations were intoxicating.

"We dated for the rest of our freshman year and into the beginning of our sophomore year. The breaking point for us was, from her perspective, my lack of concern for greater social change. It wasn't so much that I didn't care, but I was never going to be as intense as she was. I never got much into the rallies she took me to, and mostly did it for her. In the beginning she was interested in my thoughts, but they weren't enough to keep us going. Although I liked our conversations, they eventually became tiring. I wanted to do things with her like fly a kite on the beach or go to the movies. She seemed too busy with social issues and thus the contention for my "lack of zeal", as she put it. I did care, just not all the time. After our break up, I wasn't as heartbroken as I was confused. People say you generally meet a mate in college, but I was only twenty. I thought it was way too soon for me to be thinking about finding a mate.

Erick stopped for a moment. He turned to Francesca. "I hope I'm not boring you with all of this." Francesca assured him she was very interested in what he was saying. She told him he was a good storyteller. He asked how her feet were and she also assured him that she was fine to continue walking and listening.

Erick continued, "I started to hang with a new crowd. Most of them came from hippie parents. They were free-spirited. There were two guys, Frank and Tim, and a girl named Lani. I met them in my anthropology class. Most of their parents had traveled extensively and had instilled in them the importance of acceptance and open-mindedness.

"Lani was gorgeous; she was a mix of Hawaiian, Puerto Rican, and French. She was exotic to me. Although I liked Frank and Tim, Lani was the real reason I hung around. She had a vivaciousness about her that was really attractive. She liked to laugh and seemed amused by my jokes. Although she was also a sophomore, she was older than me by a year-and-a-half. She had spent a lot of time traveling and less time in class. It was her habit to take semesters off and use her financial aid checks to take trips. Her ability to travel alone was intriguing to me. I was drawn to how adventurous she was.

"In high school, I didn't do much more that smoke pot. Lani and the guys, however, dabbled with pot, hash and mushrooms. One night Tim popped open his film canister. I expected to see some green weed, but there was something else. "What's that?" I asked.

"Shrooms man."

"Shrooms?"

"Don't tell me you've never done these."

"No man, I haven't."

"Well, if you like the ganja, you'll love these, they're a real nice accent piece. It's way different. It opens up your mind, you won't be as philosophical as with pot, and your thinking will be real clear. You want a hit?"

"As long as I don't lose control." After a few puffs, I remember Tim telling me to look at this psychedelic picture on the wall. We all sat there staring at it and trying our best to pick out scenes within the picture. It seemed weird to me. I never did mushrooms after that. I much prefer the buzz of a good German stout.

"Lani was an army brat and had lived all over. As the year progressed, she and I spent more time together. Frank was salty, because I think he had a thing for her, but he never had the guts to make a move.

"She and I seemed like a perfect fit. When we weren't with the guys we spent a lot of time near the water and in the city. She loved seafood, so whenever I had the cash we would go to the wharf for dinner. Lani was big into photography. Many of our weekends were spent at the Golden Gate Bridge and I'd watch her take pictures of the awesome views.

"She was 5'5" and had wavy brown hair that she usually wore up in ponytail or bun, but my favorite was when she wore it down. She was very simple and laid back, a total bohemian. She usually wore sandals, even when it was cold. She appreciated my intensity and we rarely argued. The only thing we ever disagreed on was how she spent her money and why she was in school if all she really wanted to do was travel. Lani had no solid plan for the future. Her father chose Berkeley because he thought it was where she would fit in. Her mother was a retired nurse and her father had retired early from the military. He spent two years in 'Nam, as an officer. Lani said that her mom told her he wasn't the same when he came back. He was really aloof. He had gotten his degree in engineering at Berkeley and his daughter was following in his footsteps, except she was majoring in anthropology. Lani knew it bothered him that she was so flippant about school. Several times he threatened to stop paying for her education if she didn't buckle down. She would get scared and start being more serious about studying for a few months but then would slip back into her old habits.

"She was a gifted artist, and thought school was hindering her creativity. Her photos were amazing. She even knew how to develop her own film. With respect to our relationship, neither of us knew what we wanted at that point in our lives. She was twenty-three and I was now twenty-one and all we knew was that we loved each other. It never seemed to get too deep, which was mostly Lani's doing. I told her once that I thought of marrying her. She said, "Oh Erick, you're so silly." That was the last time I ever mentioned it.

"Lani's lack of commitment became apparent in our relationship. She never outwardly cheated on me, but was very flirtatious with other men. She didn't have an obvious way of flirting, it was more playful, but my jealous nature couldn't handle it. She would tell me that I was overreacting, and that I was possessive. I tried to explain that if the shoe was on the other foot she would feel the same, but in reality I don't think she had a jealous bone in her body. Lani and I had been dating for about ten months when I realized that it probably was not going to be much more than a college thing, and that she wasn't a woman who would settle down. She had too many things that, in her words, she "wanted to experience." When she broke up with me, in the summer before my senior year, she told me that I was too serious and that she was like a butterfly that needed to spread her wings. That is what she was, a butterfly that had to fly and be free and she felt that I was holding her back. The one thing Lani taught me was about being free."

Erick stopped his stride. "I think it's time to head back now." Francesca followed his lead. The air was damp and heavy.

The conversation made her feel close to Erick, but she did not know how to express that. She couldn't say that she had a "dream" man, but she knew a good thing when she saw it, and she was definitely taking notes. The feelings she was developing for him were real, but she was not sure what to do with them. Someone sharp-minded and intelligent was a big draw, and that he was.

Erick had suggested meeting back at the bluff in a week. Francesca could barely stand the thought of waiting that long, but fortunately her job search kept her occupied.

Chapter 7

"I don't wear flip flops in the sand or lay on a towel to work on my tan."

Their next rendezvous was now only a day away. Francesca decided to take a break from her search and head to the beach. She often sat at a lifeguard tower, despite the signs reading "Keep Off." It became her ritual to frequent these vacant towers, especially during difficult times in her life.

As she approached her tower of choice she noticed something underneath it. From a distance it looked like a dead seal, but as she neared, she realized it was a blanket, and under the blanket appeared to be someone sleeping. She paused only briefly before heading to the next tower. The sun was a phenomenal orange. She marveled at its deep, rich hues as she climbed the tower, and sat with her back propped against the wall facing the ocean. With her legs crossed she peered through the railing. Much like that of a roaring campfire, the ocean had a profound hypnotic effect on her. With the sun setting so late, beach dwellers lingered for hours as the coolness of the day began. She looked around at the several couples on the sand, some hugging, some kissing, others holding hands. The ocean was like a natural aphrodisiac. There was a man and a woman with two small children packing up their beach umbrellas, coolers, and towels. Out of the corner of her eye she saw an older gentleman approaching with his metal detector, searching for buried treasure. Nearby was a child and father duo flying a kite. She was enchanted by the sailboats and counted five that day.

The water was calm and glassy and the hues of the sunset reflected on the ocean like a painted canvas. The sound of seagulls rang in the distance. A flock of pelicans cruised by, inches above the water, one of her favorite sights. The ocean sounds, sights, and smells took her to other places where she knew no woes.

Her state of nirvana was interrupted by the sound of her name.

"Francesca?"

She turned hastily to see a familiar face.

"Erick?" Caught off guard, and unexpectedly pleased, she smiled softly and said, "This is a surprise, I didn't expect to see you until tomorrow."

"Well," He stammered a bit, "I just came down to see the day end."

"Would you like to join me up here?" she asked.

"Gladly," he cheerfully agreed.

"I was just reveling in the beautiful sunset."

"Yes, it is beautiful." Erick gazed in her direction." Realizing that his comment was directed more toward her than the sunset, she became fidgety.

"The smog is good for at least one thing, great sunsets." She laughed nervously. "How was your week?" she asked.

"Kind of dull," Erick answered.

"With work?"

"Well, uh, yeah, kind of. Francesca..." Erick was not his usual confident self, and Francesca was searching his face for answers as to why.

"What is it?" she asked.

"Here's the thing." He hesitated with a long pause. "I have not exactly been honest with you. I know we don't know each other that well, but I feel the need to share something with you."

"Go on." She sat patiently, focused on his every expression.

"When I told you I did freelance work, that was not exactly true. The reality is that...man, this is harder than I thought it would be."

"It's ok, take your time." She looked at him with compassion, despite having no idea what he was about to say.

"I'm just going to say it. Francesca, the truth is that I'm homeless, and I've been homeless for about two years now."

"You're homeless? Oh my goodness! Why? I mean, how come? I mean, wow. I don't really know what to say right now."

"That's all right, I didn't expect that you would."

"Do you need a place to stay? Can I help in some way?"

"That's really sweet. It's not that simple though," his comment baffled her, but she didn't ask anything else.

She reasoned that if he told her that he was dying or that he was moving to another state, or even something more intense like he had murdered someone, she would have more words. She couldn't understand how an intelligent, attractive man could be homeless. She always associated homelessness with mental illness or people who were uneducated. She had never met a homeless person who spoke and acted the way he did. Her head was swimming with questions. She was quiet for several moments.

"Francesca," he said gently, breaking the silence. "I know you must be wondering a lot right now. This is not exactly how I had planned on sharing this with you. As a matter of fact, I had no intention of sharing this with you because I had no intention of getting involved with you in the first place."

"I do have a lot of questions, but I'm not sure where to start. I think maybe I should go for now."

"Do you still want to meet me tomorrow night?" he asked hesitantly.

She paused before answering. It had always been virtually impossible for her not to show her emotions on her face, and she was certain he could see her bewilderment and shock. Her state of quandary was overwhelming. Perhaps it was because she had real hopes for this relationship, but now all of her fantasies were crashing down with the waves of that one word…homeless.

"Sure, I don't see why we can't meet tomorrow," she said flatly.

"I look forward to seeing you tomorrow then," Erick said with a boyish insecurity.

He knew she was disturbed by his confession and wished that he could take it back, and just for a few more moments, continue the way things had been. Still, he knew he needed to tell her before continuing on. He knew this information could very well be the end of their burgeoning relationship.

"All right, Erick, I'll see you at the bluff tomorrow, at dusk." She avoided making eye contact.

Francesca stood up and walked down the ramp making every effort not to look back at him. She accidentally glanced back momentarily only to see him waving goodbye. She hastily waved back.

She was feeling more things than she knew what to do with. She was confused, hurt, sad, and angry. She also felt cheated. She spent hours toggling back and forth between feeling slighted, then angry, and then guilty for feeling angry. She questioned why she just couldn't find someone normal. Then her need to rescue began to rear its head as she thought of ways to help him. Maybe she could start looking for jobs for him, too, since she was already in the throes of her own employment search.

Francesca tossed and turned the entire night, formulating questions, trying to regain composure. Twenty-four hours ago she had been a woman full of hope, with the anticipation of a blossoming relationship. Now she felt her world had been turned upside down. She was treading in unknown waters. "Do not fall for this guy," prevailed in her thoughts, but perhaps it was too late, because she already had.

She knew she couldn't tell anyone about this, not even Shannon. She imagined the conversation. "Hi Shannon, um, I'm falling in love with a homeless man. Oh, and we're going to spend Saturday night together. No, he is not taking me out, we are just going to spend time at the beach, talking." The thought of it was absurd.

It was close to 6:30 p.m., and they were meeting in an hour. Her thoughts were no clearer than the day prior. She spent most of her morning and afternoon doing mindless activities, laundry, grocery shopping, and organizing, all to avoid the thoughts that were yearning to surface.

She was not sure how to act when she saw him. She was tempted to be cold and calculating, but in her heart knew that doing so would be wrong. The unknown terrified her, as did the thought of being hurt, yet again.

Francesca arrived at the bluff first, just as she had hoped. Erick arrived just seconds past 7:30 p.m.

"Hello," he spoke quietly.

"Hi," Francesca replied.

"How are you?" he asked.

"I'm ok, and you?"

"I had a decent day," he answered quickly. "We should head down to the beach before we miss the sunset."

Francesca followed with a nod and walked closely behind him down the steps. In mid-stride Erick stopped and began to speak.

"I know what I told you yesterday must have been very hard for you. I just want you to know that I understand if you decide this is our last time together." His words softened her countenance.

"I appreciate you saying that. I do have several questions. I'm not sure how I feel right now."

"I understand. Let's sit so we can talk more."

They walked the entire way from the stairs, past the bike trail and to the very tower where they sat the night before, without a word. The day still had a few more moments left before the sun made its final exit. There were fewer people out, and the evening was cooler than the previous. Thick, white cumulous clouds rested on the horizon.

"All right, here we are. Are you going to be warm enough?" he asked.

"Yeah." They both sat facing the ocean.

There was a short silence before Erick started. "What are your questions?" he asked as he turned toward her and leaned in with genuine interest.

"Erick, before I start asking you questions, I need to share something."

"Ok."

"What you said on the stairs really has helped me to feel more comfortable. I appreciate you acknowledging how difficult this is for me. I have no idea the outcome of this friendship, but I need you to know that I am glad for the short time I've known you."

Deep in her heart however, she was feeling gypped. She had been really hoping for something with this relationship. She had no idea how they could continue. She felt sad at these thoughts because she had a real connection with Erick. In a very short time, with just a few conversations she was falling for him. It was undeniable. She loved how he made her feel so beautiful when he looked at her. She loved how he seemed to hang on every word she uttered, and that they had such profound conversations. She thought it may be too good to be true, and now, the unfortunate fact that that theory was proven right made her stomach ache.

"I'm not sure where to begin."

"I know this is not the easiest thing to swallow," he reassured her.

"I guess what I am wondering more than anything is, why? I mean what happened to get you to this place? You seem so together, I really don't understand. Where do you live? How do you survive?" She stopped herself. "Sorry, I know that's more than one question."

"It's all right." He smiled. "I kind of live all over, but mostly at the beach, I feel the most peaceful here. As far as eating, I do what I can. I sometimes eat at the shelter. I don't like to beg, so when times are rough and the shelter is full, I go without."

"What is the longest time you have gone without eating?"

"About a week and a half, in the very beginning, before I learned about the shelter."

"What do you do when it rains or in the winter when it is really cold?"

"When it rains I am sheltered by the lifeguard tower, and when it's cold, if I can't stand it, I'll get a bed at a shelter, but that's not my favorite. I feel stifled there. There are too many people and I don't get the same peace that I get when I'm by the ocean, so sometimes I'd just rather withstand the cold. Besides, I chose to live this way, so I don't feel like anyone owes me anything."

"Wait a minute, you chose to live this way? Now I'm really confused! Erick, pardon my being so bold, but who in the world chooses to be homeless?"

"I realize it probably sounds a little off the wall to you."

"A little? I'm really curious to hear what would cause an attractive, intelligent, charming man like you to choose to be homeless."

"It's complicated, but I will simplify it for the sake of time."

"I'm in no rush, you just opened Pandora's Box; you're going to need to shut it."

He chuckled, slightly taken aback by her forthrightness.

"Since you put it that way, I will give you the long version. You may want to make yourself comfortable. Are you warm enough?" he asked again.

"Yes, I'm perfect."

He let out a sigh, and began his story. "You are the first person I have shared this with so I need a second to gather my thoughts."

"Take your time," she reassured.

"Thanks," he nodded. Then he began, "I wasn't home from Berkeley for more than a couple of weeks when I got a call from one of the companies I had applied to. It was an advertising agency. I was pumped. I started working for the firm two weeks after my interview. I felt like a prince, the new guy, and the one with promise. I was hired as the junior graphic designer. I was the youngest among my colleagues. I kept to myself and made sure to impress my bosses with timely work and long hours. I kept this up for about six months and then started to slow down once I settled into the job. I felt successful in what I did and started to acquire stuff. I bought a brand new BMW after nine months. My pay was good and I felt like I deserved nice things. In my second year on the job, I bought a condo not too far from my parents in Santa Monica. I was living the life. I stayed focused and made it a point not to get caught up in any serious relationships. I casually dated a girl from work, and we lasted for about three months. As soon as she became too serious, I broke it off. I met another girl at the gym. We dated for about two months before I found out that she had a kid and some serious drama with the kid's father. I began to be content with being alone.

"I spent some time with my sister. She was attending UCLA, getting her degree in communications. She wanted to be a journalist. She had a pretty serious boyfriend, so most of the time we spent together was when we all met at my parents' house for our traditional Sunday dinners. I didn't have much more than this going on in my life outside of work.

"I found myself working more hours, mostly to continue to secure my position and advancement. The few friends I made at the gym or other places stopped calling because every time they asked me to hang out, I told them I was working. I was on a mission, my goal was senior graphic designer, then department head and eventually, regional manager. I thought if I worked more and performed better, I could make my way up the ladder and eventually start my own graphic design firm.

"My mother started to worry about me because I had missed a month of Sunday dinners. She called me one night and told me that she thought I was working too hard, that work would always be there and that I needed time to unwind and spend with family. She told me to get a girlfriend or a hobby so that I could be well rounded. I approached work much like I did studying, with force and drive. Once I become determined about something it is hard to be convinced of anything else. I started attending family dinner again, but when I would go I would take my laptop. She didn't like that either, but knew it was the only compromise we could strike.

Francesca shifted, inching closer to Erick. The sun was completely gone and the ocean air was thick. A slight mist started to settle around them. There was only them, their voices and the black sky, which blended seamlessly into the sea, making them indistinguishable. She shivered a bit, but hoped that Erick did not notice that she was cold. She wanted to hear the rest of the story. Erick's speech was softer than usual. She knew it must be hard to speak of these things. She got the sense that this was therapeutic for him, so she refrained from asking questions. She realized she'd drifted from his story to her thoughts for just a moment, and she once again tuned in.

She rejoined the story with him saying, "I went to the doctor for my first physical in years. The doctor looked at my chart, then up at me, then back down at my chart. He was in his early sixties, in decent shape. 'Son, how old are you?' he asked. 'Twenty-six', I said. 'I am going to be frank with you.' He had a worried look on his face. 'If you don't lower your blood pressure, your risk for a heart attack or stroke by age forty is imminent.' He asked me what I did for a living and how much I worked. I fudged the numbers a bit, because I was not ready to hear him say I needed to work less. At the time I was working about sixty-five hours per week. I told him between forty-five and fifty. 'Son', he said. 'You need to make some time for yourself. Slow down, take a vacation, practice a sport, anything, but you need to take much better care of yourself.'

"I cordially thanked him for his concern, but had no intention of slowing down. Not now, not when I had the advantage of youth on my side. I was not going to be the golden child forever.

"As time went on I started to realize I was becoming the status quo Santa Monican, Californian, American. Something I never strove for. I was working for my car and my home. I had the appearance of having it all, spending big, but having very little to show for my work. My social life was shot and I had no idea how to build it up again. The few "friends" I did have thought I was a bore. I thought I was a bore. I had no idea how to transition into this new life of professionalism without succumbing to consumption. I thought this was what all professionals did in their mid-twenties. I figured I would slow down once I built my fortune. I know that I had deviated so far from my father's standards. He was a hard worker, but never a workaholic. Everyone around me told me, indirectly, that I had a problem.

"I couldn't figure out what happened to the kid who wanted to live free and travel, the guy who didn't want to be tied down to material possessions. I felt possessed and powerless. My world was reeling out of control. I had nightmares almost every night and during the day all I could do was fantasize about the way my life would be without all the pressure. I dreamt of backpacking from country to country, meeting new people, experiencing new cultures. I thought of Lani and her free spirit. I didn't have anyone to be open with about any of this. I felt trapped, like I was suffocating, buried alive. I toyed with the idea of smoking pot or drinking heavily, but I knew that wouldn't solve my issues. The reality of it all was that the pressure was perceived. My boss never asked me to work sixty to seventy hours per week. I was the one who had become obsessed with success. I felt like there was no balance to achieve. It was all or nothing, either I continued on this path with the risk of giving myself a heart attack or I gave it all up. Unfortunately, by that point all my money was tied up in my condo and car. I had not done much to save and felt like it was much too late to start now. I couldn't go on like that. Would I quit my job and hand it over to one of the young punk interns just out of college after four years of pouring my life out for this company? Would I just disappear? I had no idea. I was stuck, like super-glued fingers."

"Wow, I couldn't imagine that kind of pressure on a job," Francesca responded.

"Yeah! I started out by calling in and requesting personal days off, then calling in and pretending like I was sick. Vacation time away was not enough. I got to the point that I dreaded going in to work, and had an enormous amount of anxiety thinking about it. One day, I just quit. I didn't' give a formal resignation or any notice. I just quit. I was not in my right mind.

"I was able to live for a little while because I had enough in the bank to cover my mortgage for about two months, but my car and other obligations went to pot. My car was leased, so I took the hit and turned it in early. I no longer paid my credit card debt, and I got to the point where I had to decide on paying bills or buying food, and food always won. I was so ashamed of what I had done and where I had gotten myself, but didn't have the strength to ante-up and look for another job. No one knew what I was doing. I didn't tell anyone, for fear that they would have me committed. I knew what I was doing was crazy, but I had no control over the anxiety. I was too proud to see a shrink. My fate was looming. I contacted my bank and voluntarily foreclosed on my house to keep some of my dignity. I remembered back to conversations I had with Lani. We used to fantasize about having no obligations, financial or otherwise. We talked about traveling to foreign lands, having just enough for food and lodging. We were going to sell artwork and make music to survive. At the time I knew it was just talk. Of course it would've been great to live that freely, but even in our fantasies I knew it wasn't realistic, and I would never, in a million years, actually do it.

"As I was allowing my life to slide into the abyss, it was these very conversations that overtook my thoughts. I imagined a place where no one would know my name, where I didn't have to answer to anyone, a place of independence from anything institutional or concrete. I imagined a sort of 'never-never' land, a place that I never had to leave. The crazy thing is, in many ways I am living out that fantasy. But for the past two years, it has been anything but a dream. At times it has been excruciatingly lonely and painstakingly difficult. My biggest regret is that I didn't go to some foreign land. I wish I would have lived out that part of the dream, traveling by boat and hitchhiking my way through life. The stark reality is that I am here in the United States living amongst a very specific community of people, most of whom have not chosen this life." Erick stopped and turned to Francesca. "I am sure it's a lot to swallow, but this is my story."

"Erick, who in the world am I to judge you. You just spilled your guts to me and I am in awe of your conviction. Still it doesn't make complete sense to me. What about your family? What do they think? How do you stay in touch with them?"

"Actually that is another regret I have." Erick's eyes became vacant as he gazed out toward the black ocean, on the verge of tears.

"I'm sorry if that's too personal, you don't have to answer."
"No, it's not too personal. It's something that I don't like to think about much, because it's painful." He continued on, "After I let all of my

credit go into default, I skipped town. My cell phone and all other lines of communication were cut off, but I knew I had to face my family. I figured no time would be a good one, so I went to them just before the holidays to drop the proverbial bomb. My father didn't even stay in the room for me to finish my story. My mother cried, and asked what she had done wrong. My sister, who had looked up to me for so many years, seemed crushed and perplexed. I have not spoken to them much since that day. I stop in to check on my mom about once every couple of months, but try to make sure my dad's not there. We catch up over coffee and she stocks me up with food. I usually don't stay for more than an hour or so. I can't face my dad. I know he is more than disappointed in me. I understand, so I keep my distance. I make sure to tell mom to tell everyone hello. As for my extended family, I don't think anyone knows. I'm sure that's how my mom and dad like to keep it. I just wish that I could still have the same relationship I used to have with my family, but I know that this decision has come in-between that. I stay local so that I can keep up with them.

"Wow, Erick!"

His face was peaceful and he appeared to have a sense of relief. Francesca was the first friend he had since his decision to live on the streets. She felt an intense connection with him. She felt a deeper respect for him. All she wanted to do was wrap her arms around him and tell him that everything was going to be all right. Instead, she sat there silently, reflectively.

"You're the only person I have spoken to about this. Thanks for listening."

"Erick, I genuinely feel honored that you shared all of this with me. It's weird, but I actually feel closer to you, like I really know you now."

"Can I walk you home?" Erick asked.

"Yes, of course."

The walk was twenty minutes, but it felt like only five to get to Francesca's front porch. Before she could take her keys from her purse, Erick pulled her close to him and embraced her, neither wanting to relinquish the other. His arms were lean and strong, and it felt like nothing could harm her. He smelled fresh, like the ocean air they had just left.

"Can I see you again?" he asked as they disengaged.

"I'd like that."

"When?" He cocked his head to the side and waited for a response.

"How about next Saturday? Same time, same place."

He agreed, "I'll see you at the bluff."

He watched as she walked up the stairs. Before she entered her apartment, he called out, "Have a good week, Francesca."

Her name rolled off of his tongue like a ballad. His eyes pierced through to her soul. As if she had x-ray vision, she could see his heart beating.

Francesca floated into her apartment, uncertain, but fulfilled. The decision she had made, to harden her heart and disconnect, had been utterly flung to the wayside. She knew she was in for the ride of her life.

Chapter 8

"Love is a hurricane, love is a storm."

Erick was like a benign drug pulsing through her veins. She couldn't get enough of him, but had to wait patiently to see him again. The week dragged on. Her job search made it feel even longer. It was an endless search for the right fit. Francesca wanted a job with enough responsibility, but not too much. She was getting to the point that she needed to take any job, because unemployment was only going to go so far.

On top of that she wasn't sure what to do about Erick. She wrestled with the fact that there was no one to talk to, no one to share her joy or her confusion. She was falling in love, but not in a traditional sense. How in the world would this work? What was she getting herself into? She had never respected a man as much as she did him. She had never felt the things that she did when she was with him. He was a man of passion and integrity, yet confused and lost all at the same time.

Friday night before the date, Francesca met Shannon for drinks on Pine Avenue at a small and unassuming club. She studied Shannon's face as she began to tell her about her burgeoning relationship with Erick. She kept it upbeat, a fun and exciting new romance. She had no intention of telling her the whole story. She had never been good at keeping things from people, especially Shannon, but she tried her best not to share too many details.

"So what does he do?" Shannon asked.

Francesca was stuck. She had not properly prepared for her questions. She reasoned that Shannon was not generally concerned with those types of things. She was dumbfounded and Shannon sensed it.

"Did I ask something wrong?"

"No, no, not at all, it's just that I don't really know how to answer that." She was stammering. She finally spit out, "He's a graphic designer by trade."

"That's a good profession," Shannon replied with no further inquiry.

Francesca was out of the woods. She couldn't believe that she escaped without making up a story. In her heart, she knew it was only the partial truth, but it would do for the time being. She wasn't prepared to divulge the whole story, especially since she had no sense of the relationship's future.

They spent the rest of the evening recalling fond memories of a trip they had taken to Atlanta the summer before graduation. When it was time to say goodbye, Shannon asked her to be careful with her heart in this newfound romance. She knew Francesca's tendency toward romanticism. While Shannon knew Francesca was unwilling to give of herself to just anyone, she also knew that if she found the "right" guy, she would most likely throw herself, full throttle, into the relationship. She didn't want to see her get hurt. Francesca reassured her that she was easing herself into this one and playing it safe, but not too safe.

Chapter 9
Surprise

Erick was at the bluff, waiting. It was nearly seven o'clock. She saw his slender figure posted against the railing with his back to the ocean. The scene reminded her of the climax of a romantic movie. She conjured up a scene in her mind and caught herself before uttering her next line.

He was poised through most of their interactions, but as she neared, he seemed uncharacteristically nervous.

Francesca spoke first. "Hi," she said, hoping to put him at ease. "How was your day?"

"I can't complain, but I must admit, this is, by far, the highlight."

Francesca smiled and the butterflies emerged. "Why, thank you," she said with a fake southern accent and a flutter of her eyelashes.

"Trust me, they aren't just words." He looked her in the eye. "Shall we?" He smiled and stuck his elbow out, encouraging her to continue with her southern bell character. She interlocked her arm within his and they sauntered down the stairs like a well to do socialite couple from a classic movie.

"I have a surprise for you. When I tell you, close your eyes."

"I love surprises!" She tightened her grip.

They neared their destination, Erick leaned over and whispered, "It's time." Francesca closed her eyes. The seagulls chanted, and the waves pounded the sand with their usual forceful rhythm. The wind kissed her cheeks and the coolness of the salty air settled just below her nose. The ocean sounded different with her eyes closed. She was grateful to know that she had the ability to re-open her eyes. However, having no sight for those brief moments was exhilarating.

"Keep your eyes closed," Erick instructed as their walk came to a halt. He gently removed her arm from his. Seconds later he said, "You can open them."

When Francesca opened her eyes, she was amazed at what she saw. There was a blanket spread out on the sand. In the middle of the blanket were two small candles surrounded by some freshly cut fruit and several pieces of chocolate. Near the edge of the blanket was a notebook.

"Oh my goodness!" were the only words she could muster. Part of her response was for the effort he made and the other for the curiosity she had about how he was able to make it all happen. "Erick, this is beautiful. It's really wonderful!"

"Have a seat ma' lady." He took her by the hand and extended his other arm as an open invitation for her to sit on the blanket.

She curtsied while holding out a pretend skirt.

They sat facing the ocean as an enormous orange sun melted into the cobalt blue ocean. The evening could not have been more romantic. Both were short on words as they watched the sunset beyond the horizon.

Francesca broke the silence with, "Erick, I'm afraid." She regretted the words the moment they left her mouth.

"Afraid of what?"

"The unknown."

"If it is unknown, what's to be afraid of?"

She let out a sigh. "I am so excited for this adventure we're on, more than you know, but I guess I'm afraid it is all too good to be true and I know I have no control over that."

"If you had control, what exactly would you do with it?"

"I don't know, I guess I would at least feel like I was in the know."

"What do you want to know?" Erick asked.

"I want to know what exactly it is we are doing."

"We're sitting on a blanket at the beach, and we just finished watching an incredible sunset."

"Cute. Are you always this cute?" She gave him a pretend mad look.

"I try," he said with a debonair half grin.

"Erick, what do you want out of life?"

"I suppose what I want is not that much different than the next

70

person. I want to be happy, and to make sure that the people in my life are happy."

"What do you want from me?" Francesca asked.

"I want your friendship and I want you to be happy with mine."

"That's all?"

"Should there be more?"

"Well, at this point I guess not."

"I had dinner with a friend last night. I told her about you."

"What did you say?"

"I told her that you were someone I was building a relationship with. She asked me what you did for a living. I felt like I was being deceptive because I told her that you were a graphic designer."

"What was deceptive about that?"

"The fact that I did not tell her the whole truth. I didn't tell her you were...you know..."

"Homeless." He blurted out and then fell silent.

She felt ridiculous for bringing any of it up. She knew she had ruined a perfectly good moment. The sun was completely gone and darkness began to settle in.

"Francesca, I know this is not an easy thing."

"I know, I'm sorry, I don't know why I brought any of this up."

"Well obviously it's important enough that you did."

"Yes, but we have not committed to anything in this relationship. I guess with the beautiful set up you have here and the romantic evening, I'm just feeling afraid. I don't know how we're going to have a relationship that will actually work. Erick, you are homeless, I'm not, think about it. How is this going to last or turn into anything that can have a future? The last several weeks have been a whirlwind. I have not felt as excited to see someone as I am to see you, but I am so scared and confused."

Erick leaned over toward Francesca and put his hand around the back of her neck. His hands were warm despite the cool air. He put his nose against hers and slowly placed his lips against her lips. It was more than a kiss. It was a gentle reassurance that everything was going to be all right. He withdrew his face and pulled her close. He put his arm around her shoulders. Reaching behind, he grabbed the book that was on the blanket. He opened the pages of the book.

"These are some words that I have written in this journal over the past couple of weeks, they all relate to you."

Francesca was nervous and excited.

He cleared his throat and then read:

"My heart beats faster when I am near you, like a greyhound at the gate ready to hear the pop of the gun. I am at a loss for words when you look at me, it feels like you have peeled every layer of my mask off and are staring straight into my soul. You tease me with your gentle browns, but know not the effect. You are to me a soft autumn breeze carrying a Monarch to its next destination, with no plans for settling."

He continued, "Francesca, I'm also uncertain about the future, but just know this, I care about you and I'm not ready for this to end. Let's take it one step at a time and not put too much pressure on each other or the relationship."

She was comforted by his words. "That's fair. Thank you so much for your poem, it was beautiful!" She felt flush, and her awkwardness was apparent. No man had ever written her a poem and expressed himself as unabashedly as Erick had. She nestled her head in his neck and they spent the rest of the evening in utter silence, listening to the sea and its beautiful message.

Chapter 10

"When love cannot separate man from woman,
does that mean you are meant to be?"

Francesca felt no separation from Erick in her being. She felt more connected to him than anyone, and she never wanted that feeling to end. However, the gnawing reality of what was true resonated in the undercurrents of her heart. She wanted to spend every waking hour with him, but she was so torn by his circumstances. How could a relationship like this last? She didn't want to ruin the beauty of what they had with worry. Erick told her that he thought it would be good for her to have some space so she could think about things.

"How much time?" Francesca asked.

"Maybe a couple of weeks," he responded. She reluctantly conceded.

Erick realized that things were moving fast with Francesca and that he did not know where things would go next. He really liked her. She was so easy to be around, so light hearted and fun, and really easy to talk to. He loved her humor and her maturity. He felt like it might be unfair to continue a relationship because of his situation, but selfishly he wanted to keep it going. In no way was he looking for a relationship, but it certainly felt good to have someone to spend time with. It had been so long since he had anyone in his life. He told her the break would be good for her, so that she could think, but in reality he needed the time to think.

Francesca's resume was posted on several headhunter sites, but she felt like it wasn't making a dent. She had applied for a position with a battered women's shelter as the Children's Program Coordinator. She also applied with several homeless shelters. Knowing her time was running out, Shannon suggested she register with a temporary agency. She considered it, although it was not her preferred option.

Over the weekend, Francesca went shopping with her mother. While it was one of Francesca's least favorite pastimes, it seemed like one of the only ways for them to spend time together. For her mother, shopping was like a sport, bargain upon bargain equaled a closet full of never or barely worn clothing. Francesca would have much preferred to spend her time listening to live music, or going to a café and people watching, while sipping on a chai tea latte. Her life's dream was to travel the world and eat exotic foods on all the continents. She and her mother thought so differently. Shopping seemed to be her mother's life desire, and ensuring that her home never had a spot or blemish.

Francesca told her there was something she needed to discuss with her. Her mother asked, seemingly disinterested, "What is it?"

"Well," she spoke to her half-listening mother who frantically filed through the endless hangers of women's blouses. Francesca glanced at the other harried shoppers, who were all within earshot and it made her uncomfortable. She asked, "Can we go somewhere and talk?" Her mother looked up from her frenzy. She could sense Francesca's trouble.

After making her final purchase they headed to the Redondo Beach Pier. Sitting in her mother's mini SUV, Francesca thought of a million ways to deliver the things she had been mulling over for weeks. She knew she had to tell someone because keeping it in was eating her alive. Still, she was afraid of being judged.

"Mom, I've met someone."

"Really?"

"Yes, he's amazing. He's smart and witty. He's talented and wonderful."

"Where did you meet him?"

"I met him near my apartment."

"Oh, he lives in your complex?"

"Well, not exactly."

"He lives nearby?"

"Yes."

"What does he do?"

"He's a graphic designer by trade."

"That's a great profession, very stable."

"Yeah." She hesitated.

"Sweetie, what is it?"

"Well, I have been trying to figure out a way to share this with you, but I feel like there is no easy way."

"What is it? You sound serious."

"We haven't known each other for that long, only a couple of months or so. We've spent several evenings at the beach talking."

"It sounds like he likes the outdoors."

"Yeah, he really does."

"What is it that's so hard to say?"

"Well, right around the time we started to get to know one another he disclosed something to me that was sort of surprising."

"Like what?" her mother inquired.

"Well, he told me that he is homeless and has been for about two years."

"Homeless? What do you mean? Did he lose his job? Where is his family?"

"His family lives in Santa Monica but he is staying in Long Beach."

"Why don't they take him in, help him out."

"It's kind of complicated."

"Is he at odds with his family?"

"Not exactly."

"So what is his story?"

"See, that's the thing." Francesca had developed a lump in her throat. She was not ready to hear her mother's response, and did not want to tell her the rest of the story. She was stalling for time and wanted the conversation to end, badly.

"Well, mom, um, it's kind of like this…he didn't exactly lose his job, he quit, and he quit because he couldn't handle the pressure he was facing. He had a really good job at an advertising firm. Essentially, he's never gone back to the work force. He foreclosed on his home and let everything go."

She said it as fast as she could, like a child taking cough syrup; hoping that the faster she spoke, the fewer words her mother would take in.

"What do you mean he let everything go?" Francesca knew exactly where this conversation was headed. She could feel her mother's anger welling up.

"He's decided to live this way."

Now, in a near rage, her mother responded. "Decided?"

Francesca tried to understand what her mother must have been feeling. But she could not help but feel completely defensive. Before she could even respond her mother continued, "Have you lost your mind? What, now are you going to become some hobo's girlfriend and live on the beach, too?"

"Hobo?! That's really unfair, you don't even know him."

"I don't have to know him to know that you are much better than that, and that you need to let this guy go, immediately, before you get any deeper into this relationship!"

"I can't believe you're being so harsh. I never said I was going to marry him. Can't I be open with you without being judged?"

"I'm not judging you. I am just being a realistic mother who doesn't want to see her daughter ruined."

"Ruined? What do you mean by ruined?"

"Francesca, all I am saying is that you cannot possibly think this is going to go anywhere, so why would you spend your time forging a relationship that is bound for a dead end!"

"Mom, to be totally honest, I really wish I hadn't said anything. I knew this is the reaction I was going to get, when really all I wanted was a little bit of understanding. Haven't you ever loved someone that other people didn't approve of?"

She was silent. Francesca liked when that happened. Her mother had a hard time reflecting on anything except for her own opinion, especially during an argument. Silence was good.

"Well, yes, I imagine I may have. Did you say love?"

"Yes, I did. I am falling in love with this man. I can see past the obvious. I see his heart, his soul."

"Well, my dear, it's your life, and I can't tell you how to live it. But I want you to know that I do not approve or agree with you going forward with this."

"Well, if that's how it has to be, I guess that's how it has to be."

They drove the entire way to Francesca's house in silence. She felt hurt and misunderstood. Paradoxically, she felt relieved that someone knew. She hoped that speaking to Shannon would be a whole different conversation.

Chapter 11

"Love is a best friend you can tell all your secrets, deep feelings, and sins and it will listen and listen and listen."

The conversation with her mother left Francesca vulnerable. It took her a week to recover, at which point she gathered up the courage to tell Shannon, hoping she would show her usual compassion and understanding. They sat down for coffee. This time she didn't beat around the bush. The place was packed with its usual patrons on their computers and listening to their MP3 players. Shannon sipped steadily on her latte. Francesca hardly touched her tea.

"Shannon," she said quietly as she stared down at her hand wrapped around her teacup. Shannon could tell by the look of concern on Francesca's face that she was about to unload a major bomb.

"What is it?" Shannon asked with genuine concern.

"Remember the guy I told you about the last time we met?"

"Sure. Erick, right?"

"Yeah, well, there is something I held back."

She looked puzzled. "Held back?"

"What I mean is that I wasn't completely honest with you when you asked what he did for a living." Shannon continued to listen. "It's true that he is a graphic designer by trade, but that is not what he is doing now."

"What is he doing now?"

"He doesn't actually work."

Francesca's face became hot and she began to sweat. Her heart was sluggishly pumping blood through her veins as the nausea began to set in. She swallowed hard and sipped her tea.

"What do you mean?"

"Shannon," she hesitated for a moment, "he's homeless."

"Really? What happened? Did he get fired?"

"Not exactly. He's not homeless because he's down on his luck or because he was let go from his job, or he is mentally ill or anything like that. He is homeless because he wants to be homeless." Shannon was silent, expressionless. "What are you thinking?" Francesca asked.

"I am not really sure what I am thinking right now. I'm just trying to let this sink in. So you mean to say that he had a successful career, decided to let it go and now lives on the streets? You're sure he doesn't have an illness?"

"Yes, I'm sure. I know, it sounds absolutely ridiculous."

"No, not ridiculous, I am just trying to understand."

"I'm not even sure if I understand. All I know is that I'm falling in love with this man, and was before I found out about his situation. Now it seems like it's too late to let it go. I've never met anyone like him, so talented, so humble and grounded, yet so adrift. I feel like he could be my soul mate, but this one thing, this one major, major thing is in the way. I don't know how to proceed, nor do I know how to have a conversation with him about my thoughts."

"What are your thoughts?"

"Well, on one hand I understand his feeling of not wanting to be caught up in society and the rat race, not wanting to be chained down to a job and feel enslaved to a paycheck, a mortgage, etcetera. On the other hand, I feel like he's wasting his talents and that he needs to be a viable member of society. Not necessarily in corporate America, but some other capacity. Simply running away to a fantasy world is not the solution."

"Why don't you say just that?"

"It's not that easy. What, am just I supposed to say, hey dude, your thinking is totally wrong. You're throwing your life away!"

"Fran, no one said you had to say it like that."

"I know, I know, but that's how it will sound to him."

"You don't know that. I'm sure you're concerned with losing him, but you know that if you don't say it you're not being true to yourself. If that's the case the relationship is doomed anyway. You obviously care about him."

"Yes, I do!" Francesca said emphatically.

"If it was me in this same situation, wouldn't you say something?"

"Yes, of course I would. You're my best friend."

"What makes this any different then? Isn't he your friend?"

"Yes." Francesca reflected. "I hear what you're saying. It's just scary because I'm not sure how he'll respond. He admitted that I am the first person he's told about this. I don't want him to lose trust in me."

"Don't you think he told you for a reason? Maybe he is waiting for you to say something. Besides if you say it coming from a place of love, maybe he'll hear it."

"Ugh! I feel like my head is going to explode. I need to think about this for a while.

"Francesca, you are a very intelligent woman and you will have the words to say, you just need the courage. The worst thing that can happen is that he gets defensive, but from what it sounds like, he must care about you as well. I have no doubt that he will at least listen and continue to be your friend. Who knows? Maybe he needs a challenge like this to get back on his feet. I know you'll make the right choice."

"Thanks Shannon. I knew you'd be the best person to talk to about this. Friends like you are hard to find."

Francesca left the coffee shop with a sense of peace, however, the anxiety of the inevitable conversation loomed. For the first time she dreaded seeing Erick.

Chapter 12

"Tough as nails, poised, well spoken. Underneath lipstick and curls,
she paves her own way, yet looks back to see if anyone takes notice."

Francesca had interviews with two non-profit agencies, one that offered art therapy services to children who had been abused, and another that worked with youth learning how to become entrepreneurs. Both seemed like a good fit for her experience working with the youth at the day camp. She was awaiting a response.

Erick was constantly in her thoughts. She thought of their last time together and how intense it was. It was her first time ever feeling that intimate and raw with someone, and without having sex. It was refreshing, since most of the men she dated expected a physical relationship. She spent the better part of her life being shut down emotionally, fearing being ridiculed for being too sensitive. He opened her up to her sensitive, feminine side. She no longer felt the need to be so strong.

She had no way of contacting him. The week-and-a-half that passed felt like an eternity.

They had not formally defined the parameters of 'space' and she could no longer stand the silence. She walked to the beach to find him. She went to their spot at the bluff. It was nearing sunset and balmy. The damp ocean air pressed against her skin. The only movement about the shore was a few couples hand in hand. The waves were reduced to a ripple with the gentle air as their conductor. She heard her name in the cries of the seagulls and reveled a while on the bluff before descending to the sand below. Her heart was clenched with the desire to find him.

She walked for a mile or so before realizing her search was futile. It was nothing more than a poor attempt at trying to find loose change in the seat of a car. She surrendered her quest and headed home. She neared the steps of her apartment and took one last look over her shoulder, longing for some glimmer of hope. She sighed and carried herself up the last few steps.

On her way home she thought perhaps he had forgotten her. Perhaps he was not interested after all. Perhaps he did not really feel the things that he recited in his eloquent poem. The disappointment of a love lost fell upon her and she began to spiral into an abyss of negativity.

She sat at the top of the stairs. "Hey kitty." She stroked Oscar as he reached the top of the stairs to greet her. "Did you miss me?" Oscar offered a sense of comfort.

"Yes, I did," a resonant voice uttered.

Francesca lifted her head and saw his piercing blue eyes looking up at her from the bottom of the steps. She melted.

"Hey," she said softly and hopefully.

Erick slowly mounted the stairs as he spoke. "I couldn't stay away. I had to see you!" Erick exclaimed.

"I wasn't sure when I would see you again! It's been days."

"Nine to be exact, and counting. May I?" Erick gestured to the spot where she was sitting.

"It is up to him," she said nodding toward Oscar. Erick chuckled and patted Oscar on the head.

"Nice kitty." He winked at her as he sat close and let out a sigh.

"What is it?" Francesca asked.

"I'm not sure, exactly, but I really missed you and have been thinking a lot about our last time together. It left an impression on me."

"Me too!" exclaimed Francesca.

"I've had to process a lot of things," he continued on. "Francesca, I have to be honest. I never thought that I would meet someone at this time in my life, and fall the way I have. I'm not sure what to do."

"I understand," she said.

"What do we do now?" he asked.

"I don't know," she retorted. She sensed his insecurity. She was not certain of how to put him at ease because she felt equally as apprehensive.

"I've been thinking about how unfair it is that you feel the need to conceal our relationship, and how unfair it is that I have nothing to offer you. I realize I cannot be a good partner to you because of these things."

"What makes you think I have been concealing this?"

"Francesca, come on, have you actually told people that you are dating a homeless man?"

"Yes, as a matter of fact I have."

"Really, and what has the response been?"

"My mother was not too thrilled."

"What about your friends?"

"I've only told one."

"What did they say?"

"She says I need to be honest with you about how I feel."

"And how is that?"

"I'm scared about a lot of things. Many of them the same as what I already expressed, but the biggest thing is that I'm not sure how to say what I need to say."

"What's that?" Erick asked.

She paused for several moments. She breathed deeply and let out a long exhale. She took his hand and began. "Erick, I just don't understand how a talented, attractive and amazing man like you can be content with living the way you are. I'm not sure what your plans are for the future, but I feel like you could be doing so many wonderful things with your life and for other people, but since you have chosen to live this way, you're not making any impact." She continued, confidently. "I know you're probably uncertain of how to be back in the work world, but I feel like you are so much more than what you are living right now."

"Francesca, there is no part of me that wants to be back in that rat race of a life. Nothing in me that wants the "American Dream." You have to understand that if we're going to be together that you need to accept me for who I am."

"Erick, I do accept you for who you are, I just think that the lifestyle that you have chosen is beneath you."

"Beneath me?" She knew she had offended him and decided to back off.

"Perhaps beneath was a poor choice of words. Erick, I'm sorry, I really didn't mean to offend you. Forget about it, we can change the subject if you want." She had never seen him so defensive.

"That's fine." He gruffly retorted. "I would like to change the subject." They sat in silence. The only sound was their breathing and some children playing in the distance. "I should be heading out now. I'll catch you later."

"Ok." Francesca said meekly as she watched him descend the steps. She felt desolate. He left so abruptly. She was left only with her thoughts. She threw herself on her bed and sobbed in her pillow. She cried for nearly fifteen minutes straight before the phone rang. She wiped the tears from her face and answered. "Hello."

"Hey Fran, it's Shannon. What are you doing?"

"Shannon." Francesca's voice quivered. "I just saw Erick. He came by the house. I tried to have the conversation with him, but it didn't go well at all. I really offended him. I'm not sure I'll ever see him again."

"Fran. Perhaps never is a little drastic. Why would you not see him again?"

"He left as a result of our conversation."

"And?"

"And, I hadn't seen him in days, he came by and I totally pissed him off by saying that I think his lifestyle is beneath him."

"Francesca, you were speaking the truth, and knowing you, I am sure it was not malicious."

"You're right, but I'm afraid that I won't see him for a long time."

"You might not, but I don't think you won't ever see him again." What are you doing right now?" Shannon asked.

"Besides crying, nothing."

"Come on, let's go get some ice cream."

"All right." Francesca agreed.

They headed downtown. It was a nice night. The air was cool enough for a jacket.

"Can I try your cake batter?" Francesca asked. They took their ice cream and walked along the bluff. Shannon continued to give Francesca words of comfort and wisdom.

A man walked up to them. "Hey, I don't normally do this, but I'm down on my luck. Would you happen to have some spare change?" Francesca dug in her pocket for the change that was left over from her purchase. She handed him a dollar. Shannon gave him some change.

As he thanked them and walked away Francesca asked. "What do you think about that?"

"Think about what?"

"Well, you know, when people walk up to you like that and ask for money."

"My philosophy is if I have it to give, I'll give it."

"Yeah." Francesca glanced down at the beach below; she could not help but think about Erick at the lifeguard tower.

"What is it?" Shannon inquired of Francesca's distant gaze.

"I have such mixed feelings right now. I used to feel like homeless people were just helpless souls, down on their luck, unable to get back up. I thought they were people without resources or family, but after meeting Erick all those notions have changed. I've never met someone who has chosen that lifestyle. It's baffling. I really don't understand and I feel helpless to do anything about it."

"I can understand that." Shannon agreed.

"When I tried to help, by saying what I thought, I only pushed him away."

"Maybe you're not in his life to help. Maybe he just needs a friend. Someone to be there for him."

"You're probably right, because my effort to 'help' failed miserably."

Chapter 13

"From one swing of the pendulum, one finds themself
in a completely different direction."

The arts agency offered Francesca a job as a program coordinator. She was thrilled and couldn't wait to begin what she felt was her new life calling. The job kept her busy, but Erick was constantly in the periphery of her mind. It had been three weeks since their last conversation. When she returned home from work, the quietness catapulted him to the forefront of her thoughts. Fall was quickly approaching and the weather was considerably cooler. She hoped he was staying warm and that he had enough to eat. She remembered him saying that when it got cold he would go to the shelter.

Later that week Francesca was overwhelmed by the desire to do some volunteer work at a local homeless shelter. Part of her felt selfish in doing so because she knew that it was, in part, a way that she could feel close to Erick. She remembered a debate that erupted in her social psychology class on altruism. The debate was spearheaded by an overly cynical student who said, 'No one does anything for anyone else, just because. There is always something to gain!' *Well that's stupid*, she thought, *of course people do things just for the sake of doing good*! But now, in her quiet self-reflection, she thought maybe he was right. She decided not to beat herself up over the matter. Whatever her motivation, only good could come from it. She signed up at the Long Beach Rescue Mission, downtown, where she served hot meals on Saturday mornings. She was overwhelmed by the number of homeless people.

"Good morning," an older African-American gentleman said with a pleasant smile. "We don't get to see pretty ladies like you here very often." His comment was genuine.

"Thank you. How are you this morning?" Francesca asked.

"Well, much better now that I've seen you." He winked.

"Have a wonderful day," she smiled.

"You do the same, Sweetness." His comment made her feel good and she happily served each patron that came through the line.

She was on her feet for about an hour serving meals and spent another forty-five minutes cleaning up. She took pride in her exhaustion because she knew she had served wholeheartedly. Her compassion for the people grew as she saw mothers with their children, young and old alike. Everyone seemed grateful.

She finished up her tasks and walked to her car. Out of the corner of her eye, she saw a man sitting on a bench on a small grassy knoll. His back was turned to her, but from a distance it looked like Erick. She second-guessed herself. *It couldn't be him. How could I have missed him in the food line?* She cautiously walked closer to check her assumptions. The nearer she got the more convinced she was that it was him. Her heartbeat quickened, and she felt a hard knot develop in her throat. What would she say? After all, they didn't end on the best of terms. Would he be cold or dismissive? She pushed through all the feelings and continued toward him.

Francesca approached with hesitation and whispered, "Erick?" He turned around slowly and glanced at her face. He then turned back around and lowered his head. From his response she assumed he was still hurt. She knew she owed him an apology. She collected the courage to ask him if she could sit on the bench with him. He agreed, with a barely visible nod.

Francesca sat for a moment before speaking. The silence was thick. She started, "Erick, I'm sure you must be pretty upset with me still. I owe you an apology for the things I said to you last month. I really hope you'll forgive me."

His expression softened slightly. He continued to sit in silence. Her words hung in the air for what felt to Francesca like a millennium. He gradually turned to her and said, "Yeah, I was mad. I've had a lot of time to think about it. But what can I expect? I guess it makes sense that people would judge me for my choice, but when it was you?"

"I know, Erick. I feel so badly about that. I've really missed you! I didn't think I'd ever see you again."

"I would have eventually gotten over it, but I just needed some space and some time," he said.

"I understand."

"So what are you doing here?" Erick asked.

"I started volunteering here on Saturday mornings. I didn't see you in the line. Did you eat?"

"No, actually I didn't make it in time, my alarm clock didn't go off." He smiled. No matter how many times she had seen it, inevitably his smile made her weak.

"Would you like to join me for breakfast? It can be a belated celebration of my new job."

"You got a job did you?"

"Yes, and I love it. I'll tell you all about it over breakfast." She was pleased that he did not turn down her offer. His humility was endearing. She took him to her favorite spot on 2nd Street, Shore House Café. Francesca ordered French toast and Erick had a Denver omelet.

"So tell me about this job of yours."

"Well, I work with several populations of people - youth, battered women and homeless families. I place volunteers at various facilities to run art groups."

"That sounds like fun."

"It really is! I like it a lot."

"That's great to hear." He leaned back in the booth and stretched out his arms over the top of the seat.

"What has been going on with you?" she asked.

"Well, not much to write home about, just surviving day-to-day. Last week I started scouting out some shelters that have beds for men. I know it is only October, but I want to make sure I have a spot when it starts getting colder."

"I've actually been thinking about that. I mean about you and the winter. How hard is it to find a spot?"

"A lot of places cater mostly to women, children and families. There are a lot fewer resources for single men. Last year I got one of the last few available spots."

"Do you make friends when you are at these places?"

"I wouldn't call them friends necessarily. There are guys I talk to, but they are not people I keep up with once I leave. You have to understand there are not many people that share my situation. Most of them haven't chosen this life. Stories range from people being evicted from their homes, losing their jobs, to losing their families. Some just get trapped because once they become homeless they start using drugs, and then the streets have them."

"Is it hard being one of the few people like yourself?"

"Yeah, I would say it is. It's really lonely. The one person I told that I chose this life looked at me like I was crazy and then walked away. The few people I have met like me don't stick around long. They're gypsies."

"How do you handle the loneliness?"

"For the first six months or so, it was hard, but then I got into a rhythm, you know, like a routine. After I wake up, my day usually consists of cleaning up, having a meal whether at a shelter or sometimes dumpster diving, which only happens when I'm really desperate. I do a lot of thinking, and when I can get a hold of some paper, I write. I spend most of my time at the beach, as you know. I exercise daily, push-ups, sit-ups, I run, but mostly walk, and by the time that's all over, it's close to dark, and without the light there's not much to do, so I turn in pretty early."

"Wow, that's cool."

"What?" asked Erick.

"Your discipline. Sometimes all I can do on a daily basis is eat and brush my teeth," Francesca responded. Erick chuckled.

"Francesca?"

"Yes."

"I've been wanting to ask you something."

"What is it?"

"You know I really respect you, right?"

"Yes."

"So when I ask you this, I don't want you to take it the wrong way."

"Ok."

"Will you spend the night with me?"

Francesca's heart fluttered with excitement. She knew he was *not* talking about sex. She knew exactly what he meant. She had fantasized about it before. What it would be like to sleep under the stars, but not at a campground like she did when she was a kid. What it would be like to experience how he lived. She felt honored that he would ask. She trusted him completely. She let out a gratified sigh and then answered.

"I would love to!"

Erick grinned. "What a relief, I really wasn't sure what you'd say. Do you have plans this evening?"

"No, I don't."

"Are you willing to make it happen tonight?"

"Yes!" she said with a huge grin.

"Great, I'll see you. Let's say 7 p.m.?"

"That's perfect. What do I need to bring?"

"Just yourself and some warm clothes."

"It's a date." She dropped him back at the bluff around noon and went home to prepare. She didn't plan on sharing this with anyone yet, if ever.

Chapter 14
Beneath the Stars

Francesca was nervous. The man she was falling in love with had just asked her to spend the night with him, at the beach, in his dwelling, under a lifeguard tower. She was beside herself as she prepared. She took a warm shower, turned on some music and drank a glass of wine, yet none of this helped to calm her nerves. The only being to whom she uttered a word was Oscar. He licked her hand and nestled under her arm while she sat on the couch in a state of catatonia.

She found the warmest clothes she owned - a pair of blue sweat pants, a long sleeve cotton shirt, and her Cal State Long Beach sweatshirt. She grabbed her long socks and a pair of gym shoes that she used for walking and running. She thought about the possibilities of the evening. Would he try to make a move or would he be the same respectful man she knew him to be? Would she be able to sleep at all or would they pass the entire evening talking? What if she had to go to the bathroom? Would it be safe? After a menagerie of thoughts she brought herself back to reality and decided she wasn't going to spoil things by thinking too much.

She laid on the couch for a short nap and woke up in a frenzy.

"It's six thirty, oh my gosh, I've got to go!" She threw on the clothes she had selected. She splashed some water on her face and fixed her hair, which sat on top of her head like a firework. She kissed Oscar goodbye and shouted, "Wish me luck!" as she scurried out the door.

Francesca made it to the bluff by 6:55 p.m. Erick was already there. She pulled out the blanket she always carried in the back of her car and headed across the street. She could tell he was excited and he made a flimsy attempt to hide it.

"Hello," he uttered with a big grin.

"Hi."

"I'm so glad you made it."

"Did you think I might not?"

"Well, yeah. I thought you might have gotten cold feet."

"Erick, one thing you should know about me, I am a woman of my word."

"Gotcha. I admire forthrightness."

"Thank you, I think."

"Oh yeah, that was definitely a compliment."

"Well, in that case, thank you!"

"Shall we?" He held out his hand. She was sure he noticed that she was trembling.

They walked down the same set of steps they walked down the first evening they spent together on the sand. There were no people on the shore. The cool fall air felt refreshing on her face. She closed her eyes briefly as they reached the bottom of the steps, in order to allow her senses to be filled with the sounds and textures of the night. This was one evening she never wanted to forget. She heard the ocean crashing on the shore, tasted the salty air and the faint smell of fish that reminded her why she loved the ocean. The sun was gone. She opened her eyes and only a few stars were visible, as night had not completely fallen. As they stepped onto the path, a couple on roller-blades whizzed by. Francesca's senses were full now, and she could focus all her attention on Erick. They walked most of the way to the tower in quiet observation, and then he stopped and turned to her with the most peculiar look on his face.

"Are you nervous?" He asked.

"A little. What about you?"

"Yes, I'm terrified!" She was shocked by his response.

"Really? I'm surprised."

"Why?"

"Well, because you always seem to be so calm about things."

"Yeah, well, this is not something I do. I have not shared my life in the last two years with anyone. I am more than out of practice, and I am bringing you to my home, under a lifeguard tower. This is completely unconventional."

"Erick, if I were conventional I would not be standing here with you right now having this conversation. I don't judge you based on what you have or don't have. I like being around you for you."

"That's a relief. Our last conversation really affected how I thought you viewed me."

"Erick, again, I really want to apologi...."

"No, Francesca, he interrupted, "You had every right to say the things you said to me. I know they were not out of spite. It's just that I had not been challenged like that in a long time, especially not by...." He hesitated.

"By what?"

He stammered a bit as if regretting starting the sentence. "By a woman," he said.

"Ahhh, I see. So it was your pride that was hurt." She laughed. They continued their stride.

"Here we are."

It was clear that he had put some effort into setting things up. The blankets were neatly laid out. There was a large flashlight on one of the corners of the blankets. He turned it on, and its reflection made the underside of the tower glow. In another corner was a jug of water, some cups, and a couple of protein bars. He gestured, "That's breakfast." Francesca smiled.

"What do I do if I need to go to the bathroom?" He showed her where he kept some toilet paper. "Well, it's sand you know, so you can just cop a squat, and then bury it, like a cat," he laughed loudly.

"Here's a bag to put any trash." It felt strange to her, yet familiar.

"It's a lot like camping," she said.

"It really is. Come, have a seat." They sat facing the ocean and listened to the waves crashing. "I feel so peaceful here, like no one can harm me. The ocean is a constant calming message. It lulls me to sleep every night, and it feels like home."

"Mmm, I can see that. It is very peaceful. I don't know what I would do if I didn't live near water. It really is awesome." There was a long pause while they reflected on each other's comments and drank deeply of the night and the waves.

Erick broke the silence. "Francesca."

"Yes."

"I'm so glad you came tonight." With Francesca, Erick felt comfortable. She was like a breath of fresh air. More than anything he felt like she accepted him.

"I was nervous coming here tonight. I wasn't sure what to expect, but I'm glad I came too." Francesca replied.

Erick gestured. "All right, get up." He took the top blanket and whisked it out from under the tower. He laid it on the sand and they laid face up on the blanket, with the prominent stars in view. The sky began to darken, and Francesca relished the fact that she felt so insignificant under its auspice.

"I have a question for you," Erick started.

"All right."

"If you could live anywhere in the world without the worry of your gender, ethnicity or socioeconomic status, where would it be?"

"That's a tough one. I think I would want it to be somewhere out of the United States, somewhere in the Mediterranean, like Italy or Portugal. I'd love to live somewhere that has a long history and lots of character."

"Nowhere here in the U.S.?"

"I've actually been to a lot of U.S. cities," Francesca replied.

"What's your favorite?" Erick asked.

"I loved Seattle. It's a close second to the beauty of California."

"What do you like most about California?"

"I like the ocean and the rolling hills, and the fact that we can lay outside by the ocean in the fall and not freeze." She turned to him and smiled.

"What do you like least about California?" he continued.

"By far, the pretentiousness. You know, the phony people and the Hollywood scene. It seems like everyone wants to be someone and everyone wants to know someone or name-drop. It's annoying. I do, however, appreciate that Long Beach is enough removed from it all."

"Yeah, I know what you mean. I grew up in Santa Monica. It used to be this real chill beach town and now it seems like it's being swallowed up by the industry. All the film studios have moved in. My parents' neighborhood used to be pretty unassuming, now there's new money everywhere. They tear down the old homes and build new ones. You know, these monstrosities that take up the entire lot, from front to back.

I couldn't handle it anymore. That's why I decided to move south to Long Beach because, like you, it feels untainted."

"What about you Erick? Same question. If you could live anywhere, where would it be?"

"I've given that a lot of thought, and have decided the only place I could live is out of this world. So I created a place I can only go to in my head."

"Tell me about it." Francesca asked excitedly.

"I will, but you have to promise you won't laugh."

"Cross my heart, I won't," she assured.

"So imagine the Swiss Family Robinson, on an island, with a huge tree house, I mean gigantic, with lots of space. My family and I would live off the land. We'd hunt, fish, gather, all that. It would be a mildly inhabited island with very few others, all living the same type of life style. No cars, no jobs, nothing, just living to survive, and enjoying all the simplicities of life. Everyone would have a role. We would make up stories around nightly campfires and entertain one another by dancing and singing. There would be no strife with the other inhabitants; in fact we would share meals together, regularly. The land would be lush and green; the climate would be temperate and mild. No real seasons, mostly staying between 65-80 degrees. The water's clear and the sun bright, not too many storms, but an occasional rain shower to keep the land fertile and cool. There's a lot more, but that's the gist."

"Wow, when can we go?" Francesca laughed out loud.

"We're kind of here now, minus the tree house. The lifeguard tower is a distant second."

"Erick, you have a wild imagination. Do you have it written down?"

"By the time it is all said and done I will have several books written."

"That's so cool."

Francesca had never felt so close to him as she did at that moment. In her mind the one thing that would have made this the perfect moment is if they were just camping for a night and that in the morning they would return to their home. She tried to shake the thought out of her head and stay in the moment, but she couldn't help but feel sad.

Chapter 15

"Not all days are rainy days."

They woke up the next morning to the sound of rain. The weather was brisk. The rain was falling torrentially. It took Francesca a moment to get her bearings. She had almost forgotten where she was. She turned toward Erick, but he was gone. She sat up, stretched and looked at the ocean. It was dark gray and the waves were large and unceasing. She waited a few moments to ensure she was fully awake before she made an effort to search for him. She called out, "Erick?" No response. She called once more.

"Erick?"

She heard his muffled voice say, "I'm up here." She briefly peeked her head out to see he was sitting atop the lifeguard tower.

"Good morning." She shouted over the rain.

"Good morning."

"May I join you?"

"Of course." His voice was warm and kind. She threw her hood over her head, and put on her shoes. She made a dash up the tower ramp.

"How long have you been awake?" Francesca asked as she placed herself next to him.

"About an hour."

"You're an early riser, what time is it?"

"I'd say it is about 7:00 a.m.," he replied.

"What are you doing up here?" she asked.

"Thinking." She was silent for a moment. She did not want to pry, but was curious.

"Oh, anything in particular?" Her question was subtle.

"Yes and no. I often sit up here in the morning to get my head right before the start of my day. However, today I am thinking of some things in particular."

"Do you care to share?"

"I was thinking about how much I enjoyed last night."

"Yes, last night was wonderful."

"I was also thinking about the fact that I have not spent the night with a woman in a long time. Thank you."

"For what?"

"Just thank you."

Francesca silently reflected on his comment. She tried to imagine what his life must be like, all alone, living on the beach. Erick had no friends or family support. He was alone. She thought about his gratitude and how that same gratitude showed up in every word he spoke, and every gesture he made toward her. It was endearing, and one of the primary reasons she was falling in love with him. She placed her hand on top of his and graciously accepted his expression of thanks.

After a few moments of silence Francesca asked, "So what's today's plan?"

"Well, I'm sure you're hungry. I have a breakfast bar for you downstairs. Do you want one?"

"Yes, I'm famished."

"I figured we should probably wait out the worst of this storm before you head back home." She became sad at the mention of leaving him.

Erick sprinted down the ramp and under the lifeguard tower to retrieve their modest breakfast. Francesca stared off at the white-capped waves. The sea reminded her of how small she was. She felt both happy and sad. She was happy about finding Erick, and sad about the reality of their situation. He returned with the breakfast bar, and they both sat and ate as they watched the turbulent sea.

"Erick." Francesca's voice was hesitant.

"Yes."

"I love spending time with you."

"I hear a but coming on."

"There is no but. I just feel sad right now."

"Why?"

"Well, for one, because I don't want this moment to end, but also…"

"Ah hah, I knew there was a but." His tone lightened the mood and she knew she couldn't share what was really on her mind.

"You were right."

She withdrew and decided not to disclose her thought. She was certain if she talked about her fears about the relationship that it would ruin the moment.

"Sorry, I cut you off." He continued his attentive gaze.

"That's all. I just don't want this moment to end."

"Well, depending on how long the rain lasts, it may be a while before it does."

She rested her head on his shoulder and stared out at the sea. There seemed to be no sign of any life, other than theirs. There were no boats or dolphins, no people, just the two of them. She could hear his heart beating. It was strong and steady. He wrapped his arm around her and stroked her hair. She felt one with him, and at that moment her sadness disappeared.

Chapter 16

"Love is the protector and defender of a long nasty fall."

There was no telling which way her heart would sway. She could have easily made a dash for it, cut it off, totally kicked him to the curb, but it was too late to do that. Their hearts were bonded. There was nothing she could do but to continue to remain in the moment and let the story unfold. He made sense. Her relationship with him was the personification of how she approached most sporting events, rooting for the underdog. She was alive with him, whole, needing nothing, yet lacking so much.

There was no stability, no talk of the future, just the moment, and the moments were incredible. Her whole mind, body and soul came alive when they were together. In the beginning he felt like a drug, but now he felt like air. She needed him just like she needed to breathe, and there was no way she could give him up.

Erick walked Francesca to her car. Leaning back against the door she reached up for another hug. She felt his breath on her forehead, his lips slowly finding their way to hers. It was the most tender kiss, filled with sincerity, love and passion. With both of his hands holding her face like a wine glass, they kissed and caressed desperately until she was out of breath. Her heart palpitated like a rhythmic conga. Erick released her and placed his hands around her waist. They looked upon one another without words. It was pure love; nothing held back, no fear or pain or insecurity, just vulnerability and intimacy. Francesca felt herself becoming emotional, but was afraid of being too transparent. She fought back the tears as much as she could, but the dam of their welling released like gentle streams of water on a rainy day window.

He wiped her face with his hands. Leaning down, he placed his lips near her ear and whispered. "I love you."

Francesca was stunned. Stammering, she asked. "Did you say…?"

Erick interrupted her. "I did."

"I……I…."

"Francesca, you don't have to respond. I just want you to know that I love you."

"Erick, I've never been in love before. All I know is that I have never felt for someone the way I feel for you. I have never told someone I love them before. I'm afraid."

"Afraid of what?"

"Of being hurt, of not knowing the future."

She sensed his frustration. "You have a hard time with being in the moment don't you?"

"Admittedly, I do. I'm sorry."

"For what?"

"For ruining this moment. It seems like I do have a knack for that. I'm sorry." She felt terrible. Here he was pouring out his heart and again, she was fretting about the future.

"Francesca, I'm not upset. I'm just making an observation. You need to learn how to let go and trust."

"Trust?"

"Yeah, trust."

"All I know is to trust myself."

"Well, I'm asking you to trust me."

His commanding tone, his non-intimidation, and willingness to challenge her was very attractive. She put one hand on his cheek and with as much sincerity as possible, said, "I trust you Erick. I trust you." He softly kissed her forehead.

"When can I see you again?" he asked.

"How about tomorrow night?"

"All right. Where?"

"Why don't you come over to my place. I'll make us dinner."

"That sounds great. I haven't had a home cooked meal in a long time!" Erick exclaimed.

"I get off work at 5:30 p.m. so let's say 7:30 p.m."

"Until then, my love."

"Yes, until then."

Chapter 17

"There is nothing like a rainy day to make you think and contemplate."

She only had a half hour before Erick arrived. Francesca decided to make her signature dish - teriyaki salmon, rice and asparagus. For dessert, Bananas Foster. The house was filled with aromas. Oscar was sleeping in his usual spot under the dining room table. She did not feel nervous. She felt so comfortable with Erick, as if they were one person, separated only by gender. His tenderness and strength were the perfect combination for her and he provided the love she had always imagined. She fought hard not to have too many expectations of the evening.

In her heart there was a secret hope that through the comforts of a home cooked meal and the warmth of a dwelling, he would be drawn back into the world of security and normalcy. His free spirit was refreshing, but she could not stand the thought of him being homeless forever.

Her thoughts were broken by a firm knock at the door. She ceased setting the table and opened door. She didn't understand how he managed to continually be on time without a watch.

"Hi there," she said cheerfully. "Come in." Erick walked through the door, slightly past Francesca. He pivoted while observing her living room. "Let me take your coat." While she removed his outer garments she asked, "What's the weather like out there?"

"It's kind of windy," he said. Francesca was feeling chatty, but Erick seemed melancholy.

"Is everything all right?" she inquired.

"Yeah, everything's fine."

She was concerned, but did not press the issue.

"Please, have a seat." Francesca motioned to the couch. "Can I get you something to drink?" She walked toward the kitchen to retrieve some glassware.

"Whatcha got?"

"Lemonade, water, and Riesling," she called from the kitchen.

"I'll start with the Riesling."

"Good choice," she said as she pulled out a bottle opener from the drawer.

"Tell me about your day," Erick said.

"After work I went for a short run, cleaned up a bit and then started prepping for tonight." She brought the two glasses of wine to the couch and offered him the bowl of mixed nuts sitting on the coffee table.

"What about yours?" Francesca inquired.

"Oh, nothing spectacular. I did some push-ups and dips, walked up and down the beach and did a lot of thinking."

"About what?" Francesca sat facing Erick with one leg tucked under the other.

Erick looked out the balcony window as he spoke. "A lot really, but mostly my family and how much I miss them." Erick replied.

"I would imagine so." She was doing her best to conceal the hope she felt from his comment.

"When was the last time you spoke with them?" she asked.

"I visited my mom about a month ago. I know she's really worried about me. The visits are sad, rather than happy occasions. But it's the only time I can just sit and talk with her without my dad around. I know that makes her even sadder. She has pleaded with me on several occasions to "come to my senses." Erick used his fingers to mimic air quotes.

"What is your response when she says that?"

"I usually don't argue with her. I try to put myself in her shoes and think how I would react. I can never get her to understand why I'm doing what I'm doing, and lately I wonder myself." He paused. Looking at Francesca he said, "Let's talk about something else."

"Ok. Well, the food's ready. Let's eat." They simultaneously got up from the couch and headed to the dining room. Oscar had moved from his spot and was now perched under the foot of an armchair in the living room.

"Wow, you went all out!" Francesca had lit candles throughout the house. There were several on the dining room table and they let off a soft vanilla aroma. The table was set for two, atop a red tablecloth. She set out plates, forks, knives, drinking glasses, and elaborately folded cloth napkins. "It smells great in here."

"I'm glad you like it," she smiled.

They stood across the table gazing at each other. Francesca's hair was down and full. She had on a teal V-neck sweater with her favorite pair of gold earrings.

"I didn't tell you earlier, but you look gorgeous."

"Thank you, Erick." She blushed.

He walked over and took her in his arms. They embraced. He pulled her away and looked at her as if he wanted to say something, but instead pulled her back and held her again." Francesca's heart was pounding, full of desire and love. She had not yet told him that she loved him. She was waiting for the right time. They sat to eat.

Erick took a few bites and marveled at how good a cook she was. He took a few more sips of wine and said, "Francesca, I'm sorry, but I'm really frustrated right now!" He said in a huff.

"Why?"

"I know why I am doing this, but I can't seem to convince anyone else. Our system is so screwed up and it's like no one sees it."

"Oh, I see it."

"What about our health care, our schools, the fact that we, as Americans, only get two weeks, standard vacation time, not to mention the way we treat our homeless? Since I've been on the streets, it's so different to see it from this perspective. Before, when I saw a homeless person, I would give him a buck or two and think to myself, 'why doesn't he just get a job?' But now, I am that guy. I talk to these people. I hear their stories. Some of them fell on bad luck, some of them never got a good education and depended on labor jobs, became disabled and had nowhere else to turn. No skills, no education, and no job equals no home, and sometimes all of that equals addiction. I'm doing what I'm doing to make a statement. But I have a choice. I have an education. I'm not mentally ill, and I don't have an addiction. We work nine to five jobs, or are self-employed, all trying for the American dream, yet people seem so unhappy, so unfulfilled. We chase shadows. I couldn't live like that anymore. It feels like my world is crashing down. Before I was in this sort of haze, like nothing mattered. But now, something matters."

"What Erick? What matters?"

"You! You matter! And it is so unfair to continue this relationship with no promise of a future for you."

"Erick." Francesca paused in silence, staring into her plate of untouched food. "Erick. I...I love you!" She raised her head and looked him in the eye. I love you more than words can express. I loved you almost instantly." She continued, on the verge of tears. "I'm afraid too. I'm un-sure, but please don't beat yourself up. This is all so unexpected, for both of us. I wasn't looking for love; I wasn't looking for anything but a job. I have a job now and it's very fulfilling. I'm not just after the American dream. I want more than that too. I truly want to make a difference. We both do. What makes you and I different from one another is that you got caught in the rat race and it killed you! You're rebelling and that's totally understandable. You don't have to make a decision right now, but you do eventually have to make one. Erick, I don't want to lose you!" She reached across the table and grabbed his hand. She felt desperate, like if she let go of his hand she would lose him.

"I don't want to lose you either, but I'm not ready!"

"Ready for what?"

"Ready to commit to the system again."

"I'm not asking you to commit to the system. I'm asking you to commit to me." Tears started to well up in her eyes along with a sinking feeling in her stomach.

Erick stood up from the table. "The only way that seems at all possible is to commit to the system."

Francesca remained seated and stared up at him. Her sadness was now becoming anger. "What are you saying? I've never asked you to commit to the system. I have not asked for anything."

"I know you haven't, but I feel the pressure, whether or not you say anything."

Francesca put her head in her hands in frustration. "My intention is not to make you feel pressure."

"I know it isn't, but let's face it, you're not going to spend the rest of your life with a bum! I can't take care of you properly right now!"

She lifted her head and looked at him, expressionless. She did not expect the conversation to go the way it had. She was just expecting to have a nice dinner with the man she loved. She was bemused and wondered if he was talking about marriage.

Francesca sat with her elbows on the table and her fingers on her temples. "Erick. Let's slow down for a moment. I think we need a break from this conversation. Let's eat, our food is getting cold and I'm famished.

"You're right. Let's eat."

Only minutes after they started eating, they heard a loud crack of thunder. Lighting storms were a rarity in southern California. Intrigued by the boisterous serenade they dashed to the window. It was pouring rain.

"Did you realize we were in for another rain shower?" Francesca asked.

"No, did you?"

"No, this is weird, because we don't usually get this much rain in October."

"Yeah, no kidding," he replied.

He joined her by the balcony window and motioned her to go outside. Francesca agreed. She loved rain.

They stepped out onto the terrace, and turning toward Erick she said, "There is something about the weather when we're together. It's stormy."

"What do you make of that?" he asked.

"I don't want to put too much on it, but it's kind of poetic," she replied.

He stood behind her and enveloped her with his body. She felt small, but safe. They gently swayed back and forth to the tune of their bodies. She closed her eyes and imagined they were married and had just finished an incredible meal with wine and dessert. She imagined that after relishing the rain he would lead her by the hand to the bedroom where they would make passionate love. She envisioned the next morning reluctantly releasing from the other's embrace. When they did finally get out of bed they would make breakfast together and plan their day at the dining table.

Francesca passed her hands over Erick's and interlaced their fingers. The rain was loud, but the only thing she could hear was his rhythmic heartbeat. She turned around and put both arms around his neck. She slowly passed her fingers through his hair. With his hands around her waist, he looked lovingly into her eyes.

"Erick," Francesca whispered, "I never want this moment to end."

"Me neither."

Erick passed his hands from the small of her back to the nape of her neck where he took her head in his hands. Pulling her face close to his he began to kiss her lips. They kissed for what seemed like hours, although it was only minutes.

With the dropping of the temperature they headed back inside and finished their meal. After dinner they sat on the couch and enjoyed another glass of wine.

"Where do we go from here?" Her question was filled with trepidation.

"I don't know. I have a lot to think about, a lot to consider." Erick knew that Francesca needed to know what their future looked like, but the truth was he had no idea. On one hand he felt badly for not being able to provide for her, and on the other he was simply enjoying the time they were having. He, unlike her, did not have expectations for the future. The only thing he was certain about was that he loved her.

"Yeah, I guess so." Her gaze was desolate.

"Francesca, I don't want you to feel insecure. My love for you is deep. I want nothing more than the best. I'm just not sure what to do."

"I understand. I don't want you to feel like I am pressuring you or anything."

"The pressure I feel is from myself."

"What can I do?" She felt desperate.

"Francesca, we are in two different worlds right now and there is no guarantee that we will ever be in the same one."

"What are you saying?"

"I'm saying that the way things are right now, this cannot work."

"Cannot work?" Francesca became defensive. "It doesn't seem like you are trying to fight for it to work. It sounds like you are just going to give it all up. What is that all about?" Francesca demanded.

She had struck a chord. He got up from the couch and moved back toward the window. He said nothing at all, just stood silently, staring outside. He turned to her, bent down, kissed her forehead, grabbed his coat, and walked out into the rain.

Francesca was bewildered. She thrust herself face first onto a sofa pillow and sobbed. She curled herself into the fetal position and continued to cry uncontrollably, her heart splitting in two. She knew there was nothing she could do to make the situation any different. She was at a loss.

They were two people, so much in love, yet there was a giant, undeniable chasm neither of them could cross. Her heart sank deeper as she heard the unceasing rain over her tears.

Chapter 18

"It walked away, it ran away, there's nothing more I need to say."

The next days were a blur. She fought back the tears as she sat at her desk trying to make phone calls to partner agencies. It wasn't until she left work that she allowed their full reign. Whenever she began to cry Oscar would leap from her arms. "Some friend you are," she'd call after him.

She couldn't do this alone, so she called Shannon, who came over right after work.

When Shannon arrived she took one look at Francesca and knew she was heartbroken. They sat on Francesca's bed and she told her everything that transpired at dinner.

"What can I do? Francesca asked.

Shannon really did not know what to tell her. She started with, "I know this is not what you want to hear Fran, but there is really nothing you can do. You have to let him come to his own conclusion and make his decision."

"So, what? In the meantime I'm supposed to sit here in darkness, and wait, not knowing what he's thinking, what he's doing?"

"Like I said, I know it is not what you want to hear, but yes, ultimately that is all you can do."

"Well, I'm not sure if I'm willing to do that."

"Fran, trying to take control is only going to push him further away and then you're really not going to get an answer."

Francesca tried her best to hear what Shannon was saying. All she wanted to do was run down to the beach, find him, and tell him how much of a fool she thought he was for letting their love go. She wanted to tell him that he was not only hurting her, but his family and that he needed to come to his senses and get his life together. She wanted to tell him how rejected she felt when he left her house so abruptly that night, and how selfish and childish he was behaving. All of these things were on her heart, but she felt like she couldn't give voice to any of them because deep down she knew Shannon was right, and she did not want to push him further away.

"Shannon, you're right, I'm thinking about so many things I want to say to him, but I know I can't. This is by far the hardest thing I've ever gone through. I want so much to take control of the situation, but I agree, it would only shut him down. I guess all I can do is give him space, but it's killing me!"

"Fran, I'm sorry. I really wish there was something I could do to make this easier."

"No, you've done plenty just by coming here and being my friend. I needed you and you came through. Thanks!"

They hugged goodbye. Francesca was left alone, once again, with the thoughts that consumed her.

For the next two weeks she threw herself into work and various projects, which provided her heart temporary relief. And when she felt like giving in to her emotions, she wrote poetry.

Longing

My heart aches. The waiting is killing my brain.

My inmost parts can barely maintain such vicious perplexities, undying dreams of revelry, love and solidarity.

My soul yearns, burns for the love and touch of a human who shares my being as if not to distinguish between.

My mind races, uncertain of the next hearts' embraces, which only cases the outskirts of the delusional surety.

My body's weak, my knees quake, ears shake at the thought
or whisper of your name. My eyes can hardly endure your
pure allure and I fall fast into a sudden collapse as I only
dream of being your queen.

She was desperate and could bear it no more. She had to find him. On a Saturday, she drove to their spot. She combed the beach. She wasn't willing to let him go without a fight. There was no sign of him and hopelessness settled in. The nights were cold. She got back into her car and drove down to the shelter. It was lunchtime and there were swarms of people. She stood still and visually scoured the line. She heard a voice from behind.

"Hi Francesca."

She spun around. She was so relieved to see his face. All she could say was, "Erick."

"What are you doing here?" he asked, surprised to see her.

"Why do you seem so surprised? You walked out of my house and out of my life without any words. It has been a month and I can't stand this silence. We need to talk!"

"You're right, it wasn't fair of me to have left so abruptly, but I felt like there was no other choice."

"Choice? Francesca felt her heart rate rise. "Is there some place we can go to talk?"

"Sure." He motioned with his finger to a park bench away from the commotion. They sat next to each other on the bench. There was an obvious space, physically and emotionally, between them.

Francesca had so much to say and was not sure where to start. She had rehearsed it over and over in her head, but nothing she had prepared came out. Instead she said, "Erick, you act like you are the only one with a choice to make. I have thoughts and desires and feelings too. You aren't the only one in this relationship."

"You're right," he said. There was an awkward silence. She was hoping he would speak for both of them, but knew she had to speak for herself.

"I'm not ready to lose you. I am not ready to let go!" she exclaimed.

"I'm not either, Francesca, but how do you propose we do this?"

"I don't know. How about I try it out?"

"Try what out?" He squinted.

"Try living the way you do."

"Francesca, what are you talking about? Are you crazy?"

"Yes, as a matter of fact I am! I don't know what else to do. You don't seem ready to live the way I'm living. Who knows? Maybe I'll really like it. The bottom line is that I want to be with you!"

"I want to be with you too, but you can't just leave everything. Are you going to quit your job, give up your apartment?"

"Well, I hadn't really thought that far. I have some vacation time coming up. Maybe I will take a week off and live with you and see."

"This is insane!"

"Yeah, it is, but aren't you willing to at least try?"

"I am, but aren't you worried about what your family and friends will think?"

"At this point, no."

He paused. He saw her intensity and knew she was serious. "Ok, then. When do you want to do this?"

"Well I have to get my vacation approved, so I will let you know next week."

"All right, meet me at my tower next Saturday."

"So, it's not too cold yet to sleep there?"

"No, I usually head to the shelter in late December."

"Ok, I'll see you next week." She kissed him on the cheek and watched him get back in line. Her heart was at peace, but her head was reeling.

Chapter 19
Gala

Francesca loved galas, the hob knobbing, the dressing up. It was her time to shine. It was different from the stage, but not all that dissimilar in that many of the people at these events seemed to put on a persona. She did well when interacting with people and knew how to work a crowd. To honor one of the largest financial supporters of homeless programs in the consortium this year, the evening would consist of a silent auction, entertainment, keynote speech by the governor of California, and a sit down, four-course meal.

Francesca spent the better part of the day recovering from the prior evening. Her emotional exertions throughout the week, and the memories of Erick had put her in a state of semi-depression, so she really did have to act that night. She had regrets, but mostly she just missed him.

She tried her best to put it out of her mind and decided to focus on the evening ahead. She was glad she did not have a speaking role for the event. It was an annual event put on by the consortium of nonprofit organizations with the sole function of creating further revenue for their respective agencies.

Francesca pulled her cocktail dress out of the closet. It was wrinkled, so she had no choice but to iron. The magenta silk dress clung to her full hips. She had not appreciated her double D's most of her life, but now that she was thirty she had a new perspective on life and her body. Generally, for events such as these, she would straighten her hair, but she decided to go au natural. Her curls hung at her shoulders, only half as long as they would be if straight. Her breasts were not the only things she began to appreciate. Through much of her twenties she worked so hard to stay thin, often dieting and exercising excessively. She realized that her curves and size-eight frame were coveted by men and women alike. She looked at herself in the mirror. Besides the puffiness of her eyes from the crying, she did not look her age. Most people guessed she was about twenty-four years old. Her skin, olive in the summer and porcelain in the winter was smooth and clear with the exception of some beauty marks. Most people had a hard time figuring out her ethnicity. People often thought she was Latina, but most were stunned to learn she was African and Native American.

Francesca examined herself. She had started eating clean over the past year and the benefits were showing up in her glowing skin. Jewel tones were the perfect complement to the contrast of her dark hair and light skin. She would stand out in the dress she had chosen.

She ran the shower hot so she could relax. She was excited about the gala, but even more excited about spending the weekend in Santa Barbara, wine tasting with Shannon.

She loaded up the car with her suitcase and laundry and headed to the Convention Center in downtown, Los Angeles. She arrived in time for the cocktail hour and check-in. The place was swarming with women in semi-formal attire and large diamond rings. She knew she was back in L.A. because of all the obvious plastic faces and bodies. She flashed back for a moment to a conversation she'd had with Erick about the pretention of southern California. She chuckled under her breath. D.C. was so different in that way. People were more aware and concerned about social and political issues rather than their appearances. She liked that she was among people who had the power to make change. California seemed like a playground; filled with people striving after toys and money, with the purpose of enhancing *themselves*. Despite her biases, she had to admit that the people with whom she was spending the evening were there to make a difference.

The evening was spectacular. With dinner at $1000 a plate and the tally of over two hundred silent auction items including art, spa treatments, vacation packages and even a Harley Davidson, the event brought in a total of $525,000. Each of the organizations in the collaboration would get a share to create a new program of their choosing.

The gala and the week was a huge success, and now Francesca could rest. It had been a long week and she was ready for the weekend. She met Shannon at her house around midnight.

"Hi Franny, how are you?" Shannon opened her apartment door wide and hugged Francesca.

"I'm pooped!"

"I bet. Let me help you with your bags."

"Thank you." Francesca let out a sigh. "Oh Shannon, I have so much to share with you."

"Well you'll have my attention for the whole weekend."

"Yes, I can't wait to get some wine and just unwind."

"Get some rest because we have to get on the road early tomorrow if we want to make the most of these next couple of days," Shannon instructed.

"Ok, I'm going to get ready for bed. I'll see you in the morning."

Francesca barely had the strength to wash her face and brush her teeth, but she managed. She slept like a baby. The next morning they headed out at 8 a.m., stopping to get gas and coffee.

"Tell me about your week," Shannon said as she gripped the steering wheel and backed out of the parking space.

"The work stuff was fantastic. Francesca propped one foot up on the seat and leaned her head back on the headrest. "I got to learn so much about the programs we support. The gala was the perfect finale, but honestly Shannon, that pales in comparison with the emotional rollercoaster I experienced this week. I swear, I thought I was over him."

"Who, Erick?"

"Yeah, this trip brought back so many memories. I reminisced and cried every spare moment I had."

"Wow, Fran, I'm sorry. You don't talk about him much, so I thought you were over him."

"It's been really hard." Before Francesca started her next sentence her eyes glazed over and she caught herself just before the tears commenced. "Shannon, there's something I was not completely honest with you about."

"What do you mean?" Shannon cocked her head to the side.

"I didn't tell you everything about our break up. We spent some time together."

"I don't understand." Shannon did her best to keep her eyes on the road, but wanted nothing more than to be able to study Francesca's face while she spoke.

"I took the entire week off work and stayed with him, at the beach, under the lifeguard tower."

"Are you serious? How come you never told me that?"

"I didn't want to tell you because I knew you would think I had gone too far. But to be honest Shannon, it was one of the best experiences of my life."

"We have a two-and-a-half hour drive to Santa Barbara. I want to hear it all."

"I knew you'd say that. I'm just afraid I'm going to break down."

"Maybe that's what you need in order to heal," Shannon reassured.

"You're probably right, but first can we stop somewhere to get some breakfast?"

"You read my mind." We'll pull over the next chance we get."

They found a quaint restaurant off the side of the road. Shannon ordered a veggie omelet and Francesca had the French toast.

"Let's hear it," Shannon prodded. "Start from the beginning."

Chapter 20
Day One - On the Beach

Francesca cleared her throat and drank down her grape fruit juice. She paused for several moments, knowing that telling her story would take her to a place where she would be forced to deal with the emotion of it all. She knew, however, that Shannon was the safest place possible for it. Still there was trepidation, especially since this would be her first time speaking of it.

"I talked to my boss first thing Monday morning about taking vacation for the upcoming week. Although she thought it was late notice, she approved it. The week dragged on like molasses. I couldn't wait to spend time with him. He knew I needed to wait for my boss' approval before letting him know if I could actually do it. Instead of going to meet him and tell him the news I decided I would just surprise him by showing up with all my gear. I packed water, snacks, and my sleeping bag. I took plenty of warm clothes, several changes of underwear and twenty dollars in cash. I thought it might have been cheating, but I couldn't stand the thought of wearing the same underwear for a week, nor did I want to be completely cashless. His mouth must have dropped to the floor when I arrived at the tower."

"Hi!" She said loudly as she approached the lifeguard tower. Erick was lying face up on his blanket.

He flipped around quickly to see Francesca walking with a backpack and sleeping bag. "Why hello there," he replied.

Francesca approached and put her things down on the sand. "I'm here." She threw up both arms and smiled big.

"I see that," Erick chuckled, "I was expecting you to come and let me know your decision, but I see you are here and ready to stay."

"I am. I got someone to take care of Oscar. I'm all set."

Erick lifted himself off the blanket and got up to greet her. He hugged her excitedly, and releasing her asked, "Are you nervous?"

Looking up at Erick, she replied, "A little, but I trust you."

"I'll take good care of you." He nudged her with his shoulder.

"I know." She laid her forehead on his chest. "So where do we start?"

"I was just about to take a walk and get some exercise. Would you like to join me?"

"Of course! Where you go, I go."

It was mid-morning, the air was warm for a November day. The sun was out and the tide was low. There weren't many people on the beach, just the way Francesca liked it. It gave her a sense of peace as it reminded her of how she experienced the beach as a child. Early in her mother's relationship with Sean, her mom would pack the car with cereal and snacks. Francesca and her sisters would pile in the car before dawn, still half asleep to head to the beach to watch Sean surf. As the recreational beach goers would arrive around noon with their coolers, umbrellas, beach towels and toys, she and her family would be leaving.

"How was your week?" She started with small talk.

"It was good. What about you?"

"I thought it would never end," Francesca replied.

"Were you anticipating this week?"

"Yes, and I couldn't wait!" She looked up at Erick and then gently slid her hand into his.

They walked north, toward the city. The sun cast shadows on all the lifeguard towers, giving them the appearance of large houses.

"Are you hungry?" Erick asked.

"A little."

"You'll be a lot hungrier by the time we get halfway through this walk. I thought we could stop by The Kitchen. Erick referred to what most people called a soup kitchen as, "The Kitchen."

"That sounds great. What's the food like?"

"Honestly, it's not half bad. I mean, nothing like my mother's cooking or anything, but tasty. Sometimes they have lasagna or spaghetti or stew, it just depends. It's coming up on the holidays, so the meals start to become more elaborate as peoples' consciences prod them to contribute more. They always try to make sure the meal is balanced, you know, with meat and vegetables, milk and bread."

"You're making my mouth water."

Erick laughed. "I love taking this walk, it allows me some time to reflect on life and my soul."

"Your soul?" She was curious to hear more.

"You know, being still and just listening to your soul. Don't you ever do that?"

"I can't say I have done that," she replied.

"Most people don't listen to their souls. They live minute-by-minute, hour-to-hour, without reflection on their lives. Before they know it, they realize that the decisions they made were based on impulse or what someone else told them, rather than based on what was in their soul."

She silently reflected on his words. "The closest I get to that is when I write poetry and listen to my thoughts and feelings."

"Well that's a huge start. At least you're reflecting on something within or some external experience that makes you stop and think."

"So how long do you listen?" Francesca asked curiously.

"It all depends, sometimes minutes, sometimes hours."

"What do you do when you get a really deep thought? Who do you share it with?"

"Usually with God."

"Really?" She was so intrigued and wanted to hear more.

"Yeah, I talk to him all the time. I share what I'm thinking, what I'm frustrated with, what I want in life, and what I wish to see changed in the world. Then I ask him for wisdom."

"There is no doubt he has given you plenty of that." Erick didn't reply, but she could tell he was flattered.

"What about you, what other kinds of things do you do to reflect on your soul?" Erick inquired.

"I write in my journal sometimes. That's usually when I have a lot going on, and I'm not sure how to sort it out. Sometimes I feel like I am writing directly to God, but I'm not sure if he hears me."

"Why do you say that?"

"Well, I guess because I'm not talking directly to him."

"I don't think that really matters. He hears you whether you talk out loud, write on paper or talk silently in your head, which is what I usually do."

She moved in closer to him and squeezed his hand slightly. Her heart was swollen with love for him.

Before long, they arrived at the soup kitchen. She was nervous at first because she felt like an imposter. She leaned over to him and whispered, "Erick, I feel like these people will know that I'm not really homeless."

He whispered back, "It's ok, you're with me. Besides, not everyone who comes here is homeless. Some people don't have a lot financially and want to have a nice hot meal every now and then." She felt relieved.

"What can I get you dear?" An older woman from behind the counter stared down. She could tell it was Francesca's first time.

"I'll have a piece of the fried chicken and mashed potatoes."
"Do you want vegetables with that?" She looked at the tray of mixed carrots and peas.

"Yes, please."

"You want a roll?"

"No, thank you."

"Here you go love." She heaped a large helping of vegetables on Francesca's plate and without looking at her again called out, "Next."

Erick and Francesca took their food and headed toward the picnic benches that had been moved inside. It was a large warehouse-like structure with an open kitchen in the back. Francesca stared at the workers. She wondered if they were paid or just volunteers. There were about one hundred and fifty people inside already and at least fifty still lined up outside. With the exception of the sounds coming from the kitchen or a mother occasionally correcting the etiquette of her child, the food hall was unusually quiet. People were focused on their food as if it were a task on a to-do list. The silence made her uncomfortable, so she refrained from speaking. There was a handful of women and children, but mostly men. People looked weathered and tired. It was a surreal experience. She had only ever been on the serving side, never on the receiving side of the line.

Erick leaned over and asked, in a low whisper, "Are you all right?" He sensed her uneasiness.

"Yes, I'm fine. Just thinking and observing." Francesca looked down at her plate and pushed some peas around with her fork.

"What are you thinking about?"

"I'm not sure if now is the time to discuss it. I'll tell you on the way home."

"Fair enough."

They finished their meal and put their plates on the dishwasher tray and walked outside into the fresh air.

As they started to walk, Erick zipped up his jacket and shoved both hands into his pants pockets. "Talk to me." Erick was intent on knowing her thoughts.

"Well, I think it was just the fact that I have never been on that end of things before. It felt really strange."

"Strange, like how?" Erick kept their pace brisk.

"I felt out of place. I felt sad and awkward."

"Why do you think that is?"

"I think I realized that I really don't know what these people go through and I felt helpless to do anything."

"What do you feel like you want to do?"

"I don't know really, but something."

"Hmm," Erick said under his breath.

Erick stopped. He leaned over and rested his arms on the railing of the bluff overlooking the ocean. The sun's position read 1 p.m. The reflection of the sun on the sea danced and glimmered like freshly polished diamonds. There were several boats out on the water, people walking below, kites flying, and children laughing in the distance. He turned his back to the ocean and leaned his body against the railing.

He looked at Francesca, who was facing him, and asked, "What do you think you can do to help these people?" She sensed a bit of annoyance in his voice, but did not want to become defensive.

"Educate them, get them off the street, get them good job training and skills so they can be self-sufficient and get back into society."

"What if they don't want help getting jobs or getting back into society?"

"Who in their right mind would not want to...?"

She stopped herself and put her hand over her mouth. Erick glared at her and turned back around to face the ocean.

"Erick, I'm sorry." She put her hand on his back in hopes that he would forgive her. I wasn't thinking when I said that. I'm sorry!"

"Francesca," he spoke her name without facing her and then paused. "Let's keep walking."

The silence was deadly awkward. She did not know how to redeem herself. She felt like such an idiot. They ended up back at the lifeguard tower. Erick told her he wanted to take a nap. Since Francesca wasn't tired she didn't know what to do. She lay down and tried to get some sleep, but could think of nothing else besides their lunch and ensuing conversation.

She decided to take a walk because she figured he would be asleep for at least an hour and she needed some time to think. She felt frustrated and sad. She was in love with a homeless man, no question. Nothing was easy about their circumstances. Not only was he homeless, but he did not want it any other way. It was only the first day of their week together and she was feeling so alone and out of place. She missed home, her bed, and her cat. She didn't know how he could do this day in and day out. For her, it was temporary. She would be back at her apartment in six days and he would still be living here, under a lifeguard tower with what seemed like no worries. How did this happen? Why did this happen? She questioned why she ever allowed herself to fall in love with such a man. She was confused about what to do, but certain she did not want to lose him.

Chapter 21
Day Two - Drums

"Franny, you're so brave. I really want to hear more." Shannon remarked. "Let's get back on the road and you can continue."

Shannon and Francesca piled back into the car, satisfied from their meals. Francesca continued her story.

———◊———

The next morning came quickly. It was day two and she already wanted a shower. She promised herself she would go at least four days. She rolled over and kissed Erick on the cheek. He stirred. Rubbing his hair she whispered, "Morning sleepyhead. Rise and shine, my prince." He smiled, leaned over, and kissed her forehead.

"How did you sleep?" he asked.

"Surprisingly well," she replied. "What's on the agenda for the day?"

Lightheartedly, he retorted, "Agenda? What agenda? See, that's a problem. You've got to let that go, at least while you're out here with me. We're going to go where the wind blows." He rubbed her arm reassuringly. The freedom that Francesca so much desired seemed rigid in comparison with the true freedom that Erick experienced.

"Erick, you amaze me. I mean, I think I am free and open, but when I'm with you, my idea of freedom pales in comparison. You're so good for me."

"I know." He winked. She smiled. They kissed.

They lay there until Erick said, "Up you go!"

"Ahhh, do we have to?" She reluctantly pulled herself up from her warm position. He grabbed her hand and pulled her out onto the cold sand and said, "Now give me twenty."

"Are you serious? Twenty what?" Francesca balked.

"Push-ups!" Erick exclaimed.

"What? It's only six in the morning, and I'm cold!"

"What better way to warm up than exercise? You do believe in exercising don't you?" he said tauntingly.

"Yes." She rolled her eyes.

"To make it fun, how about we race."

"Race?" she asked.

"Yeah, to see who can finish their twenty push-ups first." He laughed out loud. "But none of those girly ones."

"Oh come on, that's not fair," she protested.

"Fine, you can do the girly ones, but you have to make sure your chin is only two inches from the ground on each dip."

"Cool! You're on!"

They positioned themselves facing one another.

Erick started with, "On your mark, get set, go!"

Francesca counted hers out loud, but quietly to conserve energy.

"Fifteen, sixteen, seventeen, eighteen, nineteen, twenty!" She jumped up and yelled at the top of her lungs, "Hah! I beat you! I beat you!"

"Oh, yeah?"

Erick rushed her. She turned around and sprinted in the other direction to escape his pounce. It didn't take long before he caught up to her and tackled her to the ground. They rolled in the sand, wrestling for several minutes before he helped her to her feet. He dusted the sand off her clothes and out of her hair.

"Ah, man. I wasn't planning on taking a shower for at least another two days. Now look at me," she said as she continued to dust herself off.

She jumped on Erick's back and demanded he give her a piggyback ride back to the tower.

He walked them up to the top of the tower and they sat, allowing themselves to cool down from their exertions. Erick turned to Francesca, and completely out of context, asked a serious question.

"Francesca, why do you love me?"

She was slow to speak. "Why do you ask me that? Do you not believe that I love you?"

"I believe it, because I see it. But I have a hard time understanding why a woman like you would love or even want to be around a man like me."

She turned to face him, sitting Indian style. She placed her hands gently on both of his legs and looked him directly in the eyes. "Erick, I love you because you are the most wonderful man I have ever met. You treat me so kindly and respectfully. You are full of life and love and passion. You are probably one of the most intense people I know." She smiled encouragingly. "You are warm and kind and deep and like no other person I have known in my entire life. What is there not to love?"

He placed his hand on the back of her neck as they continued to fix their eyes upon one another. He turned her around and positioned her between his legs. He wrapped his arms around her waist and rested his face beside hers, breathing softly, moving his lips along the curve of her neck ever so slightly. They sat and watched the sea and listened to one another's breath.

They ate a small breakfast and spent some time talking. Francesca made a vow to herself that she would not ruin their time with any mention of fears. He read a couple of excerpts from his writings. They were his thoughts about the ways of the world and his undying frustration with its infrastructure and rigidity. His words were reflective, not bitter. She listened gladly. Later, they walked to the kitchen for lunch. She knew he didn't eat there on a daily basis, but for her sake, they did.

On their way back they heard a faint noise in the distance. As they neared, the sound became more distinct and the source came into view. It was a group of men and women, about twenty of them, in a drum circle. They ranged in age from twenty to sixty and looked like hippies.

"Hey Brother, Sister! Come join us!"

Francesca looked at Erick for approval. He smiled and nodded, took her hand and they walked over. The man who invited them was the only one that stopped playing. The others carried on, undistracted by the newcomers.

"Pick an instrument and join in. You don't need to be musicians, just have a heart and a soul. The name is Buck." He extended his hand and gave Erick a firm handshake. Buck was in his mid-fifties. He was wearing a long sleeve linen shirt slightly open at his neck and chest, revealing a small purple crystal pendant attached to a thin silver chain. His salt and pepper hair, which he wore down, sat just at his shoulders. He smelled like patchouli oil and sage.

"Good to meet you, man. I'm Erick and this is Francesca."

Erick bent down and picked up a small percussion. Francesca chose a tambourine. She felt like a true Bohemian. She followed Erick's lead as he played shamelessly. Most people were playing some sort of percussion, but there were two men with guitars. She looked around the circle with excitement and tapped her tambourine to the beat. She wondered how all these people knew each other. Regardless of the origins of the group, the spirit of the people was wonderful and she felt like she could have played all day. They played for three or four hours with fifteen-minute 'chat breaks' as they called them. The purpose was not only for refreshment, but also for people to acquaint themselves with the other band members. Francesca sat next to a woman named Gigi, short for Giovanna. She was a gorgeous brunette in her mid-thirties. She had green eyes and a natural glow. She told Francesca that she had a fifteen-year-old daughter. Francesca was in awe and told her she looked too young to have a daughter that age. She said she had her when she was twenty. "No kidding?" Francesca asked. Gigi told her that it was a college fling and that the guy wasn't ever really a part of her daughter's life. Francesca's heart sank as she listened to her story. She gave her a warm hug just in time for the next session. Francesca told her that her daughter was lucky to have a mother like her. She told Francesca that she had a beautiful smile and that any man would be lucky to have her. Francesca felt a bond with Gigi and spent every chat break talking to her.

At one of the breaks Gigi asked Francesca about Erick and who he was to her. Francesca wasn't sure how to answer. She and Erick never officially defined their relationship.

"I guess he's my boyfriend," Francesca replied.

"Why do you say you guess?" Gigi inquired.

"It's hard to explain really." Francesca pondered for a moment, not wanting to disclose too much. "We come from very different backgrounds."

"Why does that matter? Do you love him?"

"Yes, very much! I've never been in love before, but this is the real thing. I have never met anyone like him in my life."

Gigi smiled. "How old are you Francesca?"

"I just turned twenty-four."

"Sweetheart. You are young and I know you are in love. I want to take nothing away from that. Just know that if you are too different or this doesn't work out and you become heart broken, you will bounce back; there is more love out there."

There was part of Francesca that resisted what she was saying. Still, she clung to every word. "Thank you, Gigi," Francesca said with heaviness as she reflected on the weight of her words. She knew her relationship with Erick was deep and real and that they did love one another, but this was another reminder of how temporal it could all be.

The group was about to start the next session when Francesca heard Erick's voice. He was on the other side of the circle with a guitar in hand.

"Everyone, this next song is going to be a solo. Most of you don't know, but Francesca's birthday just recently passed. I was not able to be with her to celebrate, but I wrote a song. Francesca, this is for you." Francesca felt her face become flush and her heart pounded into her throat.

Your eyes so rich, like coffee from Brazil.
Your hair so dark, every one strand hanging in a swirl.
Your smile so bright, like the light from Heaven.
Your heart so kind, I couldn't stand to hurt your feelings.
Your name rolls off my tongue like the purest morning dew.
Francesca, my love, how I want to hold your hand
Francesca, my dear I need you to stay right here
Francesca, my friend, no one other than you has captured my heart
Forever, forever, I never wish to part. Take my hand and I'll take yours
and we'll conquer this dark, dark world.
Francesca...Francesca... Francesca... Francesca... You are my one and
only shooting star.
Francesca... Francesca... Francesca... Francesca... You will always be in
my heart!

The moment he uttered her name, hot tears streamed down her face. She tried to hold them in, but it was impossible. The song was sweet and tender juxtaposed with his bass-like, rich voice. Combined with the acoustic guitar, it was magical. It was as if no one else was in the circle. She got up, walked over to him, and threw herself around him. In all her life, she had never felt so complete and unabashed. She held fast to him and wept. Nothing of his way of living, nothing of her fears or doubts existed. It was just the two of them melded in love. He could not provide for her nor had she given herself to him physically, yet at that moment, she shared his soul.

That night, all of her doubts and fears vanished. Her love for him had never been that deep or that desperate. She floated home and felt only peace as the moon danced upon the waves.

———◇———

"How romantic!" Shannon raved.

"I know, he was good at that. He had this silent strength about him, you know, he was a real man, and he continued to astound me with his ability to woo me."

"I need to pull over to go to the restroom," Shannon interrupted.

"Me too. Do you want anything?"

"I'll take a green tea. We'll get gas at the next stop."

As they loaded back into the car, Shannon said. "Fran, this is so intriguing."

"I've written some of it down, but honestly this is the first time I've recounted the whole thing like this."

"Ok, let's pick up where we left off," Shannon said excitedly.

Chapter 22
Day Three - Seal Beach

They slept in the next morning. The air was cold and brisk. The wind whipped under the tower like a hawk. It was day three and although it was cold, Francesca started to feel at home in this outdoor dwelling. They stirred, but neither was ready to release from each other's embrace. She felt the warmth from his large frame. At that moment she wanted nothing more than to hear his voice. She gently brushed her head under his chin.

"Good morning, you." She waited a moment for a response.

He stirred and tightened his hold in acknowledgement.

"Need more sleep. Need more sleep." He reached one arm up in an attempt to stretch, but instead held it straight out mimicking Frankenstein. Francesca laughed.

"You're goofy."

"I know." He kissed the top of her head. "Are you hungry?" He inquired.

"A little."

"I'm starving!" he retorted.

"Do you want to walk over to the kitchen?" Francesca asked.

"Not today. We have some morsels here. I was thinking about taking another trip this morning."

"Oh yeah? I can't wait for this next adventure."

"Well, my love, that is one thing you can be sure of with me, lots of adventures."

"Yes, this I know. That is one of the reasons I love you so much."

They slowly made their way up. She stretched and yawned and got a whiff of her own breath. "Pew! I need to brush my teeth!"

Erick laughed. "Let me smell," as he forced his face toward her closed mouth.

"No way! Are you kidding?" She said with her hand over her mouth. "You'll fall over dead and then where will I be?" Erick roared with laughter.

"I'm going to head to the bathroom."

She took her time making her way to the restroom while marveling at the ocean. The sea was turbulent, and the wind persisted. It looked like a storm had just hit, but there were no clouds. She quickened her pace, as the brisk air caused her to shiver. She saw a woman by the restrooms and hoped it was the facility staff. As she approached, she realized there was a woman waiting to enter the restroom.

"Good morning," Francesca said cheerfully.

The woman was slumped over. She slowly lifted her head, barely acknowledging Francesca. She lowered her head back down and fixated on her own feet. She was a short, Caucasian woman who appeared to be about forty-five years old. She had a baby face, but the years were obvious. Her skin was worn and sun damaged. She looked back up at Francesca.

"What are you doing?" She slurred, glaring at Francesca.

"Just waiting for the bathroom." Francesca felt uneasy.

"Where are you from?" Her questions were pointed, but simultaneously disinterested. Her eyes were glassy.

"From here."

"Where's here?" she demanded.

"Around. I live in Long Beach. What about you?" She asked not because she was interested, but because she wanted to take the focus off herself.

"I'm from the moon!" She said throwing her head back with a bellicose laugh. The laughter rattled in her chest sounding as if she had smoked for decades. She seemed like she never had a sober day in her life. Francesca stood up and nervously paced as she awaited the person responsible for the ever-important task of opening the bathroom door. Her discomfort persisted.

"Hey. Hey." The woman called as Francesca rounded the building after checking the men's restroom. She figured she would have rather risked a man walking into the bathroom than to have to wait any longer. "Do you have a smoke?"

"No, sorry. I don't smoke."

"Hmph." The woman settled back into her foot infatuation.

Francesca heard another voice from behind, a much sweeter sound. "Good morning."

Francesca turned around in relief to see a young Latina, in her early thirties, with a set of keys. She could have hugged her. Not only did she bring relief from this strange woman, but for her bladder.

She proceeded to brush her teeth and freshen up, and headed back to Erick. It turned out that the woman on the wall was not waiting for the bathroom at all. She was still looking at her feet when Francesca left, and made no attempts to acknowledge her departure, much to her relief.

When Francesca returned, Erick had a mini breakfast buffet laid out. There were granola bars, muffins, and two oranges.

"Yum! Where did you get all that?"

"I've had it. I got it from the kitchen a few days ago. You ready to eat?"

"Yes!" Francesca grabbed a granola bar and one of the oranges and started to peel. She felt Erick looking at her, so she looked up.

"Erick," she said.

"Yes?"

"Nothing, I just wanted to say your name, and that last night was magical. I can't believe you wrote that song for me. It was so beautiful!"

"You're so beautiful."

She smiled and touched his chin. "So are you. You have the most amazing heart I've ever known." The moment was broken by the sound of a vehicle driving on the sand. A police officer rolled passed the tower and stopped. Francesca fidgeted and looked around at the blankets.

"Erick, it is legal to be here, right?"

"Technically there are laws that prohibit loitering, and if the officer's a jerk, he could ask us to leave."

"Has that ever happened to you before?" she asked.

"No. I'll do the talking, you sit tight." Erick went out to meet the officer on the backside of the tower.

"Good morning officer. Is everything all right?" The remainder of the conversation was muffled. Francesca was anxious to know what the officer had to say, but Erick talked to him for a good five minutes and when he came back, he sighed.

"What's going on? Do we have to move?"

"No, no it's nothing like that."

"Then what is it?" she inquired.

"Well, apparently last night there was a robbery at a local convenience store. The owner told the cops that the man ran toward the beach. They've been looking for him since about 1 a.m."

"Was he armed?" she asked nervously.

"I think so. But don't fret baby. That man is long gone."

She paused as she soaked in the word "baby". That was the first time he had used that term of endearment. She liked the sound of it and she played it in her head again, *baby*.

"How do you know that?" she asked.

"I don't for certain, but not many crooks return to the scene of the crime."

"I hope you're right."

"I'm gonna protect you. Don't worry your pretty little head."

"Well, I don't feel so pretty right now, especially after three days without a shower."

"You're gorgeous, shower or not. You are my little Indian princess." He smiled and kissed her on the lips.

"You're too kind. I don't know what they mean when they say chivalry is dead. You're the epitome."

"Ok darlin', finish your breakfast, because we're going on a little trip."

"Oooh, I can't wait! Where are we going?"

"For a little walk," he said vaguely.

"Where to?" she inquired.

"Don't you want to be surprised?"

"Yes. I like surprises, but I can't stand the suspense," she replied.

"If you must know, we are going to Seal Beach."

"Seal Beach? That's far! Are we coming back here tonight?"

"Easy, Tiger. I thought you liked adventure," he said.

"I do, but that's a really far adventure."

"What else do you have going on today?" he asked.

"Nothing." She felt badly for her response. She could tell he really wanted to surprise her.

"We don't have to go," he said in disappointment.

"No, no, no. I'm sorry! I didn't mean to respond that way. I want to go. I want to go wherever you want to go," she reassured.

"Ok, good, I'm glad." His face lit up again with the cute boyishness she so loved. "It's about seven miles one way. And we'll take our time. We can stop along the way and rest and window shop. It'll be fun!"

They packed their water, some snacks, and headed out. They started out on the bike trail because it was much easier than walking on the sand. It was about 10 a.m. It was a leisurely walk and the day was beginning to warm up. Francesca took in the sights and sounds. The seagulls were scavenging for food, bikers whizzed by, runners huffed as their feet pounded the cement. It was a normal day on the beach for most, but for her, it was the adventure of a lifetime. After all, she had not been home, in her bed, sharing the comforts she so easily took for granted, for three days! She was choosing, much like Erick, to live on the beach, and be free. She still felt a little burdened by everyday things, like where their next meal was coming from, but the thought did not consume her.

She was truly grateful to be by Erick's side. She took his hand. He looked at her and squeezed her hand in acknowledgement. Francesca realized he was not a hero because he chose this life. He was just like her in that he was trying to find himself and the meaning of life. She was trying to define herself professionally and he was defining himself through living a raw human existence. She admired and loved him for his steadfastness in keeping with his beliefs. He was his own man, strong and determined.

They had been walking for about a mile when he asked if she was ok, if her feet needed a rest.

"I'm fine," she replied.

"You're really quiet, he commented, "What are you thinking about?"

"Not much really. Just taking it all in," she said.

"All right."

She knew by his response that he didn't fully believe her. She wasn't ready to talk about her revelations.

Changing the subject, she asked, "How many times have you taken this walk?"

He chuckled to himself, and indulging her, said, "Only one other time. It was when I first decided to move to Long Beach from Santa

Monica. I wanted to know my surroundings better. I hadn't spent that much time in Long Beach before so I decided to walk to the next town. I thought it was very nice and quaint, but not the place that would be suited for my kind." He paused as he caught himself, saying *my kind*. "Anyway, he continued, "I liked it to visit, but knew it wouldn't be my home."

"Yeah, she agreed, it is a really nice place to visit. We used to take the kids from the marine biology camp on field trips down there down from time to time. It always brought back memories from my own childhood, when I was a camp participant. We would always go to *Grandmas* for candy and then get ice cream from the parlor on the corner." She removed her hand from his to wipe the sweat from her palm on her pant leg. She continued, "The big thing back then was jawbreakers. Kids would spend most of the day sucking them down to a point where they could finally bite into them without breaking their jaws." She smirked at the realization of her pun.

Erick laughed under his breath.

"I was so impatient, because I never did a good job of being able to suck my candy. I would always get fed up and start to gnaw at it. By the end of the day their jawbreaker looked like a planet that had been sawed in two."

"I didn't realize you had been down there so much," he said.

She could sense a disappointment in his realization that he was not showing her something new.

"Yes, but I've certainly never walked there, so I definitely still consider this an adventure." She clutched his hand.

They walked hand in hand and listened to the crashing waves. The air was still and had a haunting calmness as the morning hawk had subsided. The sun was beginning to feel warm on her arms. She removed her hand from his and put her jacket around her waist. His burlesque hand was a bit rough, like a man who worked. She always loved a renaissance man, someone who could use his mind to challenge her to think more deeply, a man who could use his strength while simultaneously having a soft spot for the arts and culture. She was acutely aware that this was a rare find, yet Erick possessed all of it and more. He was undoubtedly her soul mate. He was missing only one thing, a home. It troubled her day after day, but she continued to discipline herself not to think of it, to stay in the moment, a task not easily accomplished.

———◇———

Shannon interrupted. "What do you think a soul mate is, really, or do you think it is a s-o-l-e mate?

Francesca answered. "I've wondered the same thing. I believe a s-o-u-l mate is someone who not only speaks to your soul, but also completes it. I'm not sure how I feel about s-o-l-e mate. That would imply there is only one person in the world who is the right fit. Also, I don't think everyone meets their s-o-u-l mate."

"Yeah, I agree. Sorry for interrupting. Go on."

"At that point I turned to him and said, tell me more about your family."

He started. "You know I have a sister named Pam. She is three years younger than me. She is somewhat of a brain and very musical, and she's extremely athletic. She used to swim and play water polo in high school. She lifeguards on the side sometimes, just because she loves being around the water. My mom told me recently that, in addition to her surfing, she has also taken up snowboarding. I'm not surprised. Like I mentioned, we were pretty close growing up. She was my little sidekick and good for when I needed company, mostly throughout elementary school and some of junior high. I would never admit to my friends that I hung out with my sister. I guess you could say I outgrew her when I started high school. We are a lot alike in that we both are pretty cranial, but I would have to say I am far more in touch with my emotions than she is. I think sometimes she is too logical and philosophical. I can count on one hand how many guys she's dated. I think she scares them away by her cerebral nature. For the past several years she has taught music to children, primarily guitar and French horn.

"She sounds really well rounded," Francesca remarked.

"Definitely. She's a gem," Erick replied. "You know, my folks are German. My mom is first generation and my father is second. My mom speaks the language fluently and my dad gets by. My mother was nearly forty when she had me, so my folks are a little older.

"Our last name, Strong, was originally Stromm, but my dad's parents changed it when they moved to America. My mother moved here right before college because she wanted out of Germany. She had seen a lot. She was very young, but still remembers some of the holocaust. My parents have been married for forty years now. Our family is really traditional, which is so rare these days. My dad is the provider and my mother the homemaker. She taught elementary school before she had us, but my dad insisted he take care of things financially so that she could stay home with us. My mom is the best cook I know. My favorite is her key lime pie. I know I told you before that I was kind of bored with the fact that my family was a "normal" family, with little dysfunction. It was annoying to me in high school, but now I really appreciate it because in all honesty my parents are a great example of what I would want a marriage to look like. They respect each other. They never argued in front of us, and they were always united in their decision making."

Francesca listened attentively. She could appreciate what Erick was saying about his family, but it was hard for her to relate, since their families were so different.

"Well, you're not off the hook, tell me more about yours," Erick said as he looked at her intently.

She laughed. "You're funny." She bumped him with the side of her hip. I'll tell you about my family. Do you want to know about the immediate, extended, or both?"

"Both," he replied.

She breathed in deeply. "My family is much different than yours, as different as night and day really.

"That makes me all the more intrigued," Erick admitted.

"My mother had my oldest sister when she was twenty-one years old. She met my dad in North Hollywood. He was a wild Indian living day-to-day doing a lot of drugs and a lot of drinking. My mom is one of five sisters, the middle child. She grew up in Compton. At that time it was not the same city you hear about today. Neither gangs nor drugs were rampant. It was a family place, a neighborhood where blacks could have a "normal" life with decent homes and jobs. We were supposed to move with my dad to New Mexico, where he is from originally. Instead, he decided to leave us with a neighbor and said he was going to the store and never came back. My mom was crushed, but I was too young to remember. Not too long after, my mom met my stepfather when she took my babysitter to get her driver's license. Sean was her examiner. He loved my sisters and me, but was not ready to settle down. They ended up getting married in Vegas after my mom gave him an ultimatum. They separated when I was twelve. At the time we were living in Ventura and then moved to Anaheim. He ended up coming back for a while and we moved to a small town called Bloomington, in the Inland Empire. We only lived there about a year before they divorced, when I was fifteen."

By this time they had slowed their stride down considerably. The sun shone brightly and there was little evidence of it being fall.

Francesca continued, "My best memories are those during the years I was in elementary school, before life got sad and complicated. I had four other mothers in my aunts. They're so much fun. The aunt I am closest to, Shana, is gay. She came out in high school. She's super smart and ended up getting a four-year scholarship to USC. I lived with my aunt Niko and my oldest cousin Calisa during my senior year of high school because I needed a change of scenery. Plus, I think I was having withdrawals since my sisters had left for college. I was allowed to do things at my aunt's that I would never have been permitted to do with my mom. My mom's oldest sister, Jeannie, is the mystical type; she collects clowns, presses flowers and paints. Like many of us in my family, she inherited my grandfather's artistic genes. My aunt Dana is the mother of my youngest cousin, Andrea. She is the only one who was actually married before having a kid. My family is completely matriarchal and seemingly cannot keep a man around. They come and go for various reasons, some are driven away and others simply leave. Needless to say, I have some issues when it comes to believing that a relationship can actually have any longevity.

Erick looked at her tenderly. He halted their stride and grabbed both of her shoulders turning her toward him. With all the passion he had, he held her and stroked her back.

"Francesca, he said as they disengaged. I love you!" His words felt like reassurance that he was not going to be one of those deadbeat guys. He was telling her he loved her even though her family was not 'perfect', and he wanted her to know he loved her and would not let anything happen to their relationship. She wanted to believe him.

Before long they arrived at their destination. Francesca used the money she brought to buy some ice cream. They walked around and looked in the shop windows. They spent some time on the beach and rested before they made their way back to the tower.

Chapter 23
Day Four - Shower

The next day, Francesca woke up before Erick. It was a gorgeous day. The waves crashed on the shore like pounds of marbles. The seagulls sang their usual song and the air was tender. Despite that, she felt disgusting. She kept the promise she made to herself that she would not take a shower until day four. She didn't know how he did it. She supposed it may not be as bad for a man as it is for a woman. The last time she had gone that long without a shower was as a kid, camping in Yosemite. While the thought of being clean elated her, she was terrified because now she was no kid standing under a warm bag of water with her mother at the guard. Instead, she would be standing under a cold outdoor beach shower as a grown woman with no mother for protection.

She thought of her mother, about how they hadn't spoken in over a week. She left her phone at home and told her that she would be traveling with her friend Michaela to San Diego. There was no way she could tell her the truth. She thought about how things would be when she got back home and how her life would be permanently altered by the experience. She was certain she would never look at a homeless person the same again. She would now see them as soldiers, the real warriors of the streets. Fighting every day for what would be considered a given for most, combatting to find meals, struggling to find warmth, and rifling for dignity. She also came to understand the cruel reality about women on the streets and how they not only had to battle for everyday necessities, but also for their personal safety. Francesca knew she would think twice before complaining about being tired or hungry ever again.

She turned over and watched Erick as he slept. He was so peaceful, like he had not a care in the world. He always seemed so calm, never anxious or ruffled. She compared herself to him. She often felt stressed about many things; paying bills, performing at work or how another motorist was driving. She envied Erick and the fact that he didn't have to deal with all the rigmarole of a "normal" life. She coveted his freedom from these things.

He stirred, and she encouraged his awakening with a light tickle to the bridge of his nose. "Wake up sleepy head." She kissed his lips.

"Hey," he managed. "How'd you sleep?"

"Flawlessly," she replied. "There is, however, one issue."

"What's that?"

"I stink! I need a shower!" He laughed out loud. "You smell like a rose to me."

"This rose is turning into stink weed, and fast!" she said and they both laughed.

"There is a shower over at the back of the bathrooms."

"I know, but I'm nervous," Francesca retorted.

"What are you nervous about?"

"Of being cold, and most importantly, naked!" Francesca blurted.

"I will be your valiant towel warrior. Did you bring one?" Erick asked.

"Of course I did, but you can't peek."

"Fran, I'm a gentleman, I wouldn't dare look, at least not without your permission." He winked.

"Ok, meet me at the bathroom in about fifteen minutes," Francesca instructed.

"Of course, my love," he taunted as she wiggled out of the sleeping bag. "I am at your service."

She made her way to the restroom with her towel and other toiletries and hoped to God she would not encounter the drunk woman who was there last time. Fortunately, her "friend" was not there. She took off her clothes and exchanged them for a large beach towel. She brushed her teeth, then poked her head out to see if Erick was making his way over to the shower. He hadn't yet. She examined herself in the mirror. Her skin was softer than usual. She reasoned it was from all the moisture and salty air. She felt insecure before the week because she had put on a couple of pounds. However, now all of that was gone. She heard his voice at the door, "You in there?"

"Coming!" She scurried as she gathered her things and put her towel back on.

She was incredibly nervous. Neither of them had seen each other in the nude, and she hadn't planned on changing that. She crept out of the bathroom and made her way to the other side of the building. He recognized her timidity.

"It's okay Franni, no one is around. It won't take that long and you'll feel much better. Besides, you have my word that I won't look." Her hesitation was eased as she continued toward him. With his back to her, she handed him the towel. He took the towel in his arms and opened it as wide as possible.

She took the liquid soap out of her bag, put one hand on the knob of the shower to spray enough water to get a little lather. Since the shower did not have a steady stream, she had to continually press the button. It took about twenty-five times before she was completely clean. By the time she was done, she was shivering from the cold water and air. Erick handed her the towel and she whisked off into the restroom.

She met him back at the tower, feeling good and clean.

"Thank you so much, I really needed that. Thank you also for helping me feel secure. You're a good friend." She smiled and hugged him.

They spent the rest of the day relaxing at the beach, talking, and enjoying the day.

Chapter 24
Day Five - Conversations

One of the things Francesca loved so much about spending time with Erick was their ability to converse about a wide array of topics. Their outlook on the world and society was very similar, especially with respect to the state of the country. However, Erick's solution to these ills was much more radical than hers. He believed people needed to organize and mobilize in order to create waves on issues directly affected by the government, like the financial system, education, and homelessness. Admittedly these were new found convictions because in college he was much more laissez faire. Francesca's stance was much more moderate and evoked more of a systematic, sustained, and controlled approach. Nevertheless, no matter how each decided it best to approach the tribulations, they agreed that something needed to be done.

It was the fifth day and they were settling into a comfortable rhythm. Every morning Erick knew that Francesca would be hungry around 8:30 a.m., so he always made sure that breakfast was ready. Francesca knew Erick needed time to think and reflect throughout the day, so she gave him his needed space. Their system was flawless, yet the reality, that the time would soon come to an end, began to overtake Francesca. She felt that no matter where she was or how she was living her life, she wanted Erick by her side.

After eating breakfast they walked up to the top of the lifeguard tower and sat on a blanket, wrapping it halfway around themselves. The morning was unusually still. The ocean was like glass and the reflections of the few morning clouds were pronounced. There were few birds out and no people. They owned the beach. It was splendid.

Erick, still looking out at the sea, asked Francesca an odd question. "What do you think is the single biggest issue in our country?"

She was stumped because there were so many issues that needed to be addressed.

"Gosh, I really don't know how to answer that. There are so many, it's overwhelming." She listed off several. "There's education, healthcare, the environment, but I don't know if I can just choose one. What do you think?" she asked.

Erick pondered Francesca's question for a moment. With his finger on his upper lip and his thumb under his chin, he sat and thought. Francesca felt like he 'knew' the answer and was simply testing her. "Apathy. I think the greatest issue in our country is apathy. Very few people even care about the issues you just mentioned. The ones who do care do the best they can, but are grossly outnumbered by those who couldn't care less. And those people who the issue does not affect would never lift as much as an eyebrow to do or say anything about it. We leave it up to our politicians to make decisions about issues that affect us all, but most of them are governed by special interest groups and lobbyists. It's all a money game, and whatever industry contributes the most money to the candidate in question, that is who they're making the laws for. So why is it that the people stand aside and do nothing to promote change?"

"Wow Erick, I never really thought of it like that before."

"Fran, people like you and me are few and far between. So many Americans wake up in the morning with one thing on their minds, themselves. If they have a family, then it's themselves and their family. How much money they make, how much more money they want to make, how much money they have to contribute to their child's education, how many vacations they can take over a lifetime, how clean their cars are, how big their house is. Beyond this, there is not much more. I have seen it and lived it first hand and it makes me sick."

Francesca could see the disgust in his eyes. It bordered on bitterness. If it went unchecked it could easily consume him. "What do you think your role in all this is?" she asked gently.

"You know, I'm not really sure. That is what I spend much of my reflection time on, but I feel stumped and helpless, sometimes hopeless."

Francesca pondered. "It's a dilemma, but why do you feel so responsible to change any of it?"

"I'm not sure about that either, but the burden feels heavy."

"Do you feel like you are carrying it alone?" she asked.

"Most of the time I do. I feel like part of my being out here, living like this, is to figure it out. Figure out my role in it all. The one thing I know is if I do go back, it will never be the life I left."

It was the first time he mentioned "going back". It gave her a sense of hope, albeit cautious. She did her best not to display any emotion in response to his comment, which was hard, since she felt sheer delight.

Then he asked her a question that completely caught her off guard, "Francesca, what do you think your purpose is here on earth?"

She let out a nervous laugh. "What a question! How am I supposed to answer that?"

"Carefully, I guess." He waited.

Francesca sat in silence, staring out at the expanse of the ocean. It was vast, so much so that her eyes could not take it all in. She thought about other lands beyond the horizon and she understood why people once thought the Earth was flat. It was clear to her that even while many societies had made so many technological advances, peoples' desires and basic needs had not changed much. People needed to be fed, clothed, sheltered and loved. She thought of the countless explorers who had sailed these same seas and how many of them lost their lives with the mission to conquer foreign lands or to protect lands they possessed. She pondered about what she wanted for her future and how college drastically changed her childhood views on money and power. She was quickly coming to the understanding that she had a deep desire to make a difference in the world. Even with all of these contemplations she could not conjure up an answer that would satisfy him or herself. She continued to stare blankly, wishing that the question had never arisen. The only response she could come up with was another question for him.

"Erick, once again, I'm stumped. I don't know how to answer that. What do you think your purpose is?"

"That's a realistic response. I, too, am still trying to figure that out. I think part of my purpose is to educate and inspire people to be a part of the change our country and the world needs." He watched the sea. He had a way of communicating with the ocean that seemingly only they understood. Francesca had witnessed this conversation on several occasions. Glaring relentlessly, as if on a quest for answers to questions that, much like buried treasure, might never be found. She dared not disturb him during these moments. She entertained herself by looking at the few seagulls that emerged as they danced gleefully through the air. The wind was beginning to pick up and the once glassy surface of the ocean became a rippled mass, like the gentle lines of corduroy. Waves began to crash and the sounds of the sea developed into its ever-changing yet constant symphony. Five pelicans glided effortlessly, closely cropping the waves but in their customary grace, left them untouched. She had secretly hoped to see a seal or some dolphins.

Just then Erick returned to full consciousness. It had only been a few minutes, but during that time Francesca was certain endless notions had run through his mind.

"Welcome back." she smiled. He returned the smile with a silent gratitude for not disturbing his moment. They spoke to one another with their eyes. It was unlike any feeling Francesca had ever experienced. It was true intimacy, which only came from an honest relationship. Erick and she were friends, there was no doubt about it, and they trusted each other. Her heart swelled with the realization that he loved her simply for her, but it was almost too much to bear. She felt her eyes start to water as she rested her head on his shoulder.

He whispered in her ear, "We are going to be okay, aren't we?"

She briskly lifted her head and stared into his eyes and said, "Yes, we are."

The air was thin and cool on her lips. He inched forward and pressed his lips against hers. It was a tender kiss, full of reassurance and depth. They continued in silence, making love with their eyes.

He broke the silence with, "Francesca, I have never known any woman as patient and understanding as you. I feel like I can completely be myself with you, without any judgment."

"I feel the same way, Erick." She caressed his face which was scruffy with long facial hair. It made him look older. She liked it. His hair was now almost past his shoulders. He would cut it on occasion with a pair of scissors he kept, but since Francesca told him she liked it long, he continued to let it grow.

They turned back toward the water and watched the waves roll in one by one. The hue of the water was different that day. It was aqua in color, which was rare. After the third set of waves, Erick asked if she wanted to get up. Francesca agreed. As they arose they saw one of the most amazing sights, six dolphins surfing in on one large wave. Francesca was frozen with amazement and then let out a loud cry of delight.

"Oh my gosh, Erick, look, look! That is so amazing!" The scene only lasted for seconds, but was phenomenal. "I have never seen anything like that in my life, I can't believe that just happened. Have you seen that before?" she asked.

Enchanted by her excitement, he picked her up and threw her on his back. They galloped down the beach like a horse and damsel in a playful trollop through the sand. Francesca was utterly delirious from the scene. The remainder of the day was spent talking about other social issues. There were a few disagreements about how they would tackle these issues. She always loved a healthy debate.

Later that evening, since the moon was so bright, Erick suggested they take a walk. The ocean playfully danced beneath the moon's glare as if it were on a stage under a spot light. They initially started on the soft sand until Francesca complained of her ankle. She had gotten the injury in college from running the stairs in her jogging class. Erick motioned that they walk closer to the water since the sand was more even. The air was warmer than usual and Francesca took off her shoes to allow her feet to feel the water between her toes. Looking down, she noticed an unusual light under her feet. Initially, she thought it was the moonlight, but it persisted with every step she took. She quickened her pace and started to jog, realizing that the light was following her.

"Erick, do you see this?" she was puzzled.

"See what?"

"Watch my feet when I walk. Do you see that light?" she asked again. "Look, it does it when you walk too!"

Francesca walked closer to the water and took a handful of it. As she did, the same aqua color they saw in the wave with the dolphins was still apparent.

"Oh my goodness, it's bioluminescence!" she exclaimed. "We taught the kids about this at the marine biology camp, but I've never seen it in real life." She continued to pick up handfuls of water, splashing them toward the sea.

"Man, the last time I remember seeing this, I was about ten years old," Erick reminisced.

Francesca brushed her hand across the top of the water and a trail of turquoise followed. She splashed it at Erick. "This is the best day ever, first dolphins, now this!" She was beside herself.

He took a handful and splashed her back, saying, "Oh yeah? Two can play that game." He charged at her and she fled, screaming. She boomed with laughter as each step in the water was an illumination of color. It was as if someone were shining a flashlight from under the waves. He caught up to her and picked her up in his arms, then walked shin deep into the ocean and threatened to drop her.

"No, Erick. No! Don't, please," she pleaded playfully.

He put her down and she splashed him once more.

"That's it. You're going in!" he hollered.

She laughed uncontrollably, pleading for him not to.

"Nope! You're done for."

She stopped her laughter and said excitedly. "I have an idea. Why don't we both go in?"

"Oh no you don't. You're not going to use that one to get out of this."

"Seriously," she retorted. In order for him to realize that she was, indeed, serious, she started to peel off articles of her clothing. First her jacket, then her shirt, then the tank top she had layered underneath. Next, she unbuttoned her pants. Erick said nothing as he stared at the body he had yet to see in its fullness. She kept her bra and underwear on. Without breaking her gaze from his face she began to back into the water. First to her ankles, then to her shins, she was up to her knees before Erick came out of his spell.

He said. "No way can I let you do that all by yourself." He took off his jacket and shirt, then his pants. She marveled at his chiseled arms, chest and abs. He galloped playfully into the water making large splashes. He scooped her up and she threw her legs around his waist. He dunked both of them into the water until they were completely wet. She jumped down then onto his back and they ducked under several illuminated waves.

Fully drunk on nature, Francesca stumbled out of the water and grabbed her clothes. Erick followed closely behind. They arrived back at the tower, threw down their clothes and collapsed onto their make shift beds, rolling and tumbling around. She reached up and passionately kissed him. He kissed her back. Despite their wet bodies and the coolness of the air all she could feel was the heat of his body against hers. It was the first time she had felt this type of desire for him. With her legs wrapped around his waist they continued to kiss. She could feel him swelling between her legs and the pressure felt good against her skin. He took his hand from her face and traced it along her waist, then to her thigh, pulling it tighter around his waist. He let go of her leg and traced his hand back up toward her breast. Placing his large hand on one, he began to gently, yet firmly, caress it. Francesca was fully aroused and whispered, "Erick." When she realized what was about to happen she stopped kissing him and placed her hands on his sides. She pulled her legs down from his waist and nudged him off of her.

"What's the matter, Fran?"

"I can't, Erick. We can't."

"How come?" Erick looked at her with confusion. "Did I do something wrong?"

Francesca lay silently. She thought back to the men she had been with, how so many of them just wanted her body, just wanted a conquest. She knew that was not Erick's intention, but she could not help how she was feeling. She thought about the likelihood that if they did, their relationship would change dramatically, and not for the best. She also reasoned that if she became pregnant, she had no recourse. What would she do, raise a child on her own? Would he, at that point, choose to lead a normal life and if so would he resent her for what might seem like a trap?

"No Erick, you didn't do anything wrong. I love you and I want to, but I just can't." She rolled over and cried silently.

Erick was baffled. He got up and went to the top of the tower and sat. He loved Francesca and she loved him, so he couldn't understand how they had gone from gleefully playing in the ocean to almost making love to her silent treatment. This was the only thing, in his mind, that was missing from their relationship. He wanted nothing more than to be intimate with her. He couldn't help but feel a little rejected. He returned about thirty minutes later to find Francesca asleep.

Chapter 25
Day Six-Melt down

Francesca awoke. It felt like midnight. The air was cold and damp, her skin still salty from their swim. She didn't realize she had fallen asleep. She felt badly about letting things get so far and then stopping. She hoped Erick wasn't angry with her. She didn't want to ruin their last night together. The week had gone so well and she was proud of herself for keeping in the moment and not talking about the future. Yet, she became overwhelmed and a sense of dread came over her. She knew nothing would be the same in their relationship after that week. One of them would need to make a very hard decision. While it felt tempting to leave everything behind to be with him, she was still not convinced this was the life she wanted. He was what she wanted, but it came at a high price. The only hope she could cling to was his comment about 'going back' to a regular life. While it seemed hopeful, it felt distant.

She was not tired enough to fall back to sleep. She kept rehearsing what she would say to him. It started with, "Erick, you know I love you right? You know I want to be with you? I need to ask you something." No further thought materialized, just those three phrases over and over. She was on edge.

He must have felt it because he woke up, turned over and asked, "Fran, are you ok?"

She remained silent.

He sat up and leaned over to see that her eyes were open. "What's wrong?"

The moment she began to speak, she burst into tears, and they flowed freely as she talked through choked speech. "Erick, I don't want to lose you and I feel like I am going to. I know that after tonight, we only have one more day together and I cannot bear it. I feel like if I say anything that resembles a plea for you to come back to my world you will totally buck, but if I don't say anything, it will eat me up inside. I don't know what to do. I have never felt this way for someone before!" She was crying so hard she wasn't sure if she was even making sense.

Erick did not utter a word for some time. When he did he said, "Francesca, did you think that you staying with me for a week would convince me to leave this lifestyle?"

"I don't know. Did you?" She retorted, referring to him thinking that she would have been converted.

"I don't know what I hoped. I just wanted to spend time with you!"

"So you mean to say you had no expectations."

"No, not really," he replied.

"I find that really hard to believe. Did you think that we could go on living like this, back and forth with no commitment, me coming to visit you at the beach, and you occasionally coming over for a meal and that it would actually work?" She was fuming. "This is not a game Erick, this is my heart!"

"Franni. Why are you so upset?"

"Why aren't you upset? Are you not afraid of losing me?"

"Do you think I don't care?" he asked patiently.

"No, I don't think you don't care, but I also don't feel like you have a plan."

"A plan? Who said I was supposed to have a plan? I didn't plan to fall in love with you. I didn't plan to have to make a decision like this."

"Regardless, Erick, of whether or not you planned to have a plan, the time has come where choices need to be made. You, or me, or both of us need to make a decision."

"Whoa! Slow down, will you? Take a deep breath."

"Erick, don't patronize me."

He laughed nervously. "I'm not patronizing you. I've never seen you like this and I don't know how to respond."

"You can start by not laughing." She got up and put on her clothes and shoes. "I need to take a walk." She walked briskly up the beach with tears pouring down her face. Her walk turned into a trot and then a full out run. When she was far enough out of his earshot, she let out a huge scream. "Why?!?!?" She was talking to the air. She was talking to God. She was talking to anyone who would listen. Her frustration and fears had built up so much that she was no longer able to have a civilized conversation. *Why was he so selfish? How could he let her go without a fight? Why was all of this coming out now, on their last night together?* She had no answers.

She heard his voice behind her. It sounded small because of the distance and the waves. He called her name several times, but she did not slow down. She felt if she kept running she would not have to deal with the situation, but he finally caught up to her. He grabbed her arm and spun her around. He embraced her as she continued to sob into his chest. He stroked her hair and held her tightly.

"Francesca, what can I do so that you know I love you and do not want to lose you?"

Through her tears she just continued to say, "I don't know, I don't know!"

He picked her up in his arms like a newborn and carried her all the way back to the tower. Her sob became a whimper and it persisted until they returned. He put her on the sleeping bag that had been her bed all week and cradled her in his arms. That was the last thing she remembered before she saw the light of dawn.

Chapter 26
Day Seven

The next morning Francesca felt completely embarrassed and ashamed for her behavior the night prior and wished she could erase the entire scene from both their memories. She lay awake for some time before she stirred. She did not want to face him. It wasn't long before he awoke. She closed her eyes.

Erick rolled over to see if she was coherent. Brushing her temple he said, "Are you awake?" She did not respond. Despite this, he started to speak. "I realize you may be embarrassed about last night, and while I was completely taken by surprise, I'm not upset with you. I just wish you had expressed some of this a little sooner. I do care and I do understand this is hard, and it puts you in a really awkward position. I have thought about it many times and still do not have an answer. I want this to work as much as you do, Fran. I don't want to lose you either." He paused. "Please say something."

She turned over and with tears in her eyes, said, in a faint, barely audible voice, "What do we do?"

Erick was perplexed. He was silent for a moment. "I….I don't know." It was the first time he was without an answer. He repeated, "Francesca, I really don't know."

She sat up. They both faced the ocean. It was a foggy morning and the ocean was hardly visible. She heard only the sound of crashing waves, which collided like cars on the sand. No birds, just the haunting clamor of the sea. The fog persisted, and seemed to darken not only their view, but their hearts as well. They sat in silence and tears for some time, holding one another, listening to the waves, separately reflecting on the week and on their relationship.

"How did we get here?" Erick asked, breaking the silence.

"I don't know," she replied.

"I don't regret any of it. Francesca, you have changed my life."

She made no response. She knew he had changed her life too, but she was hurt and her pride prevented her from saying anything about that.

"Where do we go from here?" Erick asked. Neither wanted to speak of the possibility of things coming to an end.

"We still have a whole day together. Do we have to make a decision now?" Francesca asked.

"No, we don't. I want to spend this day as if there were no decisions to be made at all. The only decision I want to make at this moment is do we want to go to the kitchen?"

"Yes, I'm famished and I can really use a hot meal," Francesca said.

"Me too," Erick agreed.

They walked to the shelter in no time flat. She knew it would be her last meal on the receiving line. Perhaps she would go back on a Saturday to volunteer. Perhaps she would see some familiar faces and maybe someone would recognize her. Yet, there would be no conversation about the fact that she looked familiar.

They ate in silence with heavy hearts. His natural jovial nature was ladened with sorrow, and when she dared look, she could see the sadness in his eyes.

After breakfast, they walked back to the tower. He sat on top of the tower; the fog had lifted so the ocean was visible. She laid face down on the sleeping bag looking toward the bluff, trying to cope with the fact that she would be leaving this place soon, never to return the same. She was uncertain what would become of the two of them. She felt only dismay.

He came below and laid face up on his sleeping bag. "So I guess we should talk about something now," he started.

"Yeah, I guess so." She continued to look out at the bluff. "You first."

He gave a courtesy chuckle and inhaled deeply, then exhaled. "I don't know where to start."

"Let me help you. I know that you love me and I love you and that neither of us knows what to do," she said coldly.

"Fran, come on, I need you to look at me and not pull your heart back right now."

She rolled her eyes and turned over onto her back. They were both face up looking at the underside of the tower. He turned over and propped his head onto his hand and placed the other on her stomach.

"Fran, I'm not trying to decide anything on my own here. We're a team, right?"

She groaned. "I know, but this is just too hard for me. It would be easier if you would just make a decision."

"You know that's not fair," he retorted.

"I know, but I'm horrible at this kind of stuff."

"Well, practice on me."

She gave him an evil eye. "What is that supposed to mean?"

"Nothing. It doesn't mean anything. But let's be realistic, I'm not exactly a catch, you know what I mean? I know there are tons of men out there that would die to be with you, and here you are, with a bum, literally."

"Erick, I chose you because I saw past the fact that you live on the beach and have your meals at a soup kitchen. But I also know that you have so much more to offer and not just to me, Erick. This is not all about me. I'm talking about what you can offer the world. I know you want to make a difference. Sure, you don't want to live the life you left behind, but you can start over. You can do the things you say you want to do."

"Actually, I really do believe that now, and I have you to thank, but I'm not there yet and I don't think it would be fair to ask you to wait for me while I try to figure it all out." There was more silence. She wondered how long she would have to wait.

"How long are you thinking?" she asked.

"That's just it, I don't know."

Francesca let out a sorrowful sigh. She knew in her heart he was not the only one that needed to make a decision. She was livid, angry that the entire situation had come to this. She knew he was powerless to comfort her. Fiery tears coursed down her face. She turned over and buried her head in the pillow so he wouldn't see her anger and disappointment. They were both powerless. She was heartbroken and could speak no more.

He placed his hand around her waist and buried his face into the back of her head. He kept saying, "I'm sorry."

Francesca's heart was split in two. One part of it was going to be left behind on the beach, forever. There were no words he could have said that would have alleviated the pain. Time would be the only remedy, and it felt like not even eternity could heal her broken spirit.

She lifted herself from the pillow, regaining her composure. The sinking feeling persisted in her stomach. She turned back toward the bluff as she prepared for the inevitable moment of her ruling.

The words felt forced, like a cat taking a bath. She positioned herself to look directly into his eyes.

"This is the hardest thing I have ever had to say in my life. I'm not even sure where to begin. I know the decision lies with me and that makes it even worse. Erick, it's true that we both love each other and I realize that both of us wish things were different. I have no idea what the future will bring, but it would probably be best to take a break. I think you need time to figure out what it is you are going to do and I need to give you the space you need." Her words seemed as unsure as a wooden suspension bridge over a one thousand foot gorge.

He was gracious in his reply. "I understand." She had expected him to say more. They embraced each other while she wept.

Francesca gathered her things while he took a walk to the edge of the shore. After she finished, she watched him in the distance. He was engulfed in thought. She wondered what he was thinking. Was he disappointed? Hurt? She didn't know, because for the first time, he did not say. She tried to control her tears and knew she needed a solitary place before she could unleash the dam.

Erick walked Francesca to her car. They spoke not a word until they reached the door. They hugged for a long while. Her hands aimed to remember the curvature of his back and the strength of his neck. Her heart was trying to memorize the pulse of his. Letting go was the hardest part, and she wished it would never end.

"I will see you," he said. She was not sure what he meant by that. Would he visit her? Were they just going to be friends? The ambiguity of the comment tormented her. She got into her car and continued to look up at his face as he watched her put on her seat belt and start the ignition. He placed his hand on the window and she reciprocated. He stepped back from the car and turned to walk back down the stairs. Francesca watched him until she could see him no longer. The moment he was out of sight, she wailed as if she had lost him to death.

She wasn't sure how she made it home through all the tears. She let herself in and Oscar greeted her at the door, as was his custom. She picked him up and held him close. He was her only comfort. He had been with her through the entire thing. She lay with him on the couch and held him as she cried herself to sleep.

Chapter 27

"What if the morning never comes, what if the darkness presses on?"

Francesca knew she had to go on with her life. She was left with no sense of the future and was quickly catapulted back into the reality of her job and her responsibilities. Erick had taken her on a whirlwind adventure; an existence she had no idea was possible. There was part of her that regretted her decision on the beach that day. What would her life look like if she had taken the leap and grasped the very freedom she had always longed for? She knew she would not be able to live like that without him. With him it seemed liberating, but the thought of it under any other circumstance only frightened her.

It had been three weeks since she left him on the beach. She thought of him daily. Work was her only relief, but even then he was in the back of her mind.

"Shannon, that's when I called you. But obviously I only told you part of the story; that we had broken up. I remember the conversation like it was yesterday. You asked me about how long it had been since we had last spoken, and I told you it was three weeks. I told you that I cried every day and it felt like someone had died. Then you told me you knew I loved him, but that maybe I needed to let it go. I thought, *let it go? Let it go? Was she out of her mind?* I remember telling you that I loved him and did not want to lose him. Then you told me it seemed like I already had lost him because he was clear that he was not ready to give up his life. I don't know what irked me more, your flippant response or that cliché, but I was fuming. Then you told me that neither of us was in a place to compromise and that I may as well simply cut it loose. I guess I just thought that you, of all people, would be a little more understanding. That's when I excused myself from the conversation under the guise that I needed time alone to think."

"Fran, I'm so sorry. I had no idea you were feeling all of those things about that conversation. I hope you can forgive me for being so insensitive," Shannon replied.

"Of course I forgive you. It is partially my fault since I didn't disclose everything. How would you know how much I was really going through? That night after our conversation, I didn't sleep a wink. The next day at work, I could not focus. I asked to take a mental health day. My boss' compassion almost brought me to tears. I couldn't just let it go without seeing him one last time. I drove straight from work to the beach. It was a hazy day. Sometimes I enjoy that type of weather, but that day it only reminded me of my own gloom. I sat in my car for several minutes rehearsing what I would say to him when I saw him. I made up several scenarios. Perhaps he would be happy to see me or maybe upset and cold. I thought through all of my responses for the different scenarios and then mustered up the strength to walk down to the tower. It was cold, and though he may have been in the shelter in the evenings, I knew he would be at the beach during the day. I was not dressed for the beach, but knew I had no time to waste. I had been thinking about seeing him for weeks. The air was moist and thick. It left the taste of salt on my lips. I saw a man with a metal detector in the distance. My heart raced faster and faster as each step brought me closer to the tower. As I approached I noticed there were no blankets under the tower, no sleeping bags, no papers or backpack. It was completely clean.

"My heart dropped. I was not giving up that easily. Maybe he decided to move his things or maybe they were at the shelter. I thought perhaps he didn't want to be in the same spot that we spent time together because it would have been too hard. I walked north, on the sand, and checked several of the towers for any sign of him. Then I walked south. Nothing. I rushed back to my car and went downtown to check the shelters. Even though I pleaded and assured the man at the mission that I knew Erick, he said he could not give me any information on who checks in and out of the shelters.

"I was perplexed. Had he relocated completely? I knew he would not go to Seal Beach. Maybe he moved up to Santa Monica, but according to him, there were too many homeless people there and the city was saturated with services. He liked his solitude too much.

"I headed back home, defeated and desolate. I began to write in my journal, because I felt there was nowhere else to turn. I began with, "I have lost the love of my life, I think, forever.

"I wrote and cried for hours. I wrote about the things he taught me, about the way he made me feel. I wrote about each day on the beach that we spent together and how free I was with him. I wrote about how smart he was. I wrote about how judgmental people can be toward someone like him without even beginning to understand the real person. I wrote about all of the social ills we discussed and knew if he put his mind to it he could be part of the solution. I wrote and wrote and wrote and wrote because I knew that this was the only way I would ever keep him close to my heart. I wrote as a tribute to his courage and strength.

"I knew I might never hear from Erick again, at least not in the literal sense. But whenever I was tempted to change someone's thinking, I would catch myself and remember how I could not change him. When I passed a homeless person, I would make sure to give whatever I had to give. I continued to volunteer at the shelter, in my heart hoping to see him. My love for him propelled me to continue to do good. I had much more desire to be a part of the political process. I knew Erick would think me too moderate, but nonetheless, be proud. It was the one small way I could continue in his desire for change.

"He was the only love I had ever known, a love so free, so genuine, so powerful. Some evenings, I would imagine a knock at my door, hoping for him. He was a refreshing breeze in my menagerie of confusion and self-discovery. He was my savior from subtlety and complacency. Still, when the summer wind blows and I smell the ocean I can feel him. He will always be my soul by the sea."

Made in the USA
Las Vegas, NV
15 January 2024

84410646R00104